RECKLESS ENDEAVOR

DAVID EBRIGHT

WELCOME TO THE WORLD OF JACK RACKHAM
AND THE SEQUEL TO

BAD LATITUDE
A JACK RACKHAM ADVENTURE

Copyright 2018 David N Ebright

ISBN 978-1-7322277-3-6

Printed in the United States of America

The characters and events in this book are fictitious. Any similarity to real persons, living or dead is coincidental and not intended by the author.

Photo Credits: Deb Ebright
Book Cover Credit: SelfPubBookCovers.com/FrozenStar

STAUGUSTINEPUBLISHING.COM 2018

RECKLESS ENDEAVOR IS DEDICATED TO

the memory of my wonderful parents…

my wife, Deb—who is always there…

and my grandkids—I love being your "Pop"

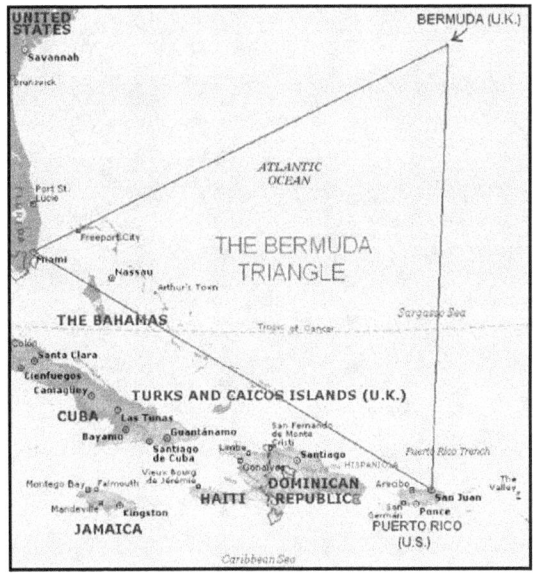

THANK YOU

DEB (my awesome wife)—incredible photographer, motivator, beta reader, and best friend (love you lots) —AKA "Nan"—my inspiration

CRISTI TAIJERON at Endless Horizon Designs for her work on layout, design, publicity and marketing. Also an outstanding author and publisher—she really "gets" pirates!
www.endlesshorizondesigns.com

JESSE GORDON at A Darned Good Book— great to work with—attentive—knows his stuff.
adarnedgoodbook.com

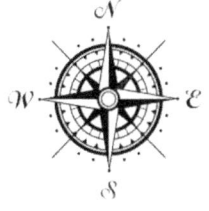

RECKLESS ENDEAVOR

NOVEMBER, 1720
GALLOWS POINT
PORT ROYAL, JAMAICA

.

❧ X ❧
PROLOGUE

❧A THICK ROPE made of hemp and flax cinched his neck, biting into the skin while a thinner cord bound the gnarled hands behind his back. Calico Jack Rackham, condemned to suffer a pirate's death, stood weak-kneed on a wooden platform in the blistering heat facing the sea, his weight supported atop a trap door. When the flap fell away, he would plummet into the void beneath the gallows. He prayed that his neck would snap with the plunge, rather than strangle in agony while blood vessels and capillaries burst and hemorrhaged.

In the sand, twenty yards away, lay the gibbet, an iron cage made from flat bars curved and wrapped to match the physical dimensions of the doomed pirate. It would be suspended from a makeshift yardarm posted at the entry to the wharf and encase Rackham's corpse for two years while scavenging birds fed on his rotting, stench-ridden carcass until only bleached white bones remained. The display would serve as a warning to buccaneers everywhere that the authorities governing eighteenth-century Jamaica punished piracy swiftly and brutally.

His arrogance and love for mischief, Rackham decided, had been his downfall, as he reflected on the events leading to his predicament. Eighteen months earlier, he had accepted a full pardon from Governor Rogers by renouncing piracy, determined to settle into life as a law-abiding citizen. His resolve lasted only a few short months. Restless, broke and hopelessly in love with the daughter of a domineering plantation owner, Jack had convinced Anne Bonny to run off to sea with him and take up the lifestyle that fed his cravings for freedom, wealth and adventure.

Rackham and Bonny assembled a crew of ruthless battle-hardened sailors, stole a sloop named *The William* and, from their hideout nestled within a deep-water cove among the islands of the Bahamas, began a reign of terror throughout the waters between Hispaniola and Bermuda. Over the course of ten months, they commandeered dozens of ships carrying priceless cargoes belonging to Britain and Spain.

As Rackham's notoriety grew, his hunting grounds dried up, forcing the dreaded pirate and his crew to target the azure seas surrounding Cuba and the northern coast of Jamaica where the ship flying the black flag with the white skull centered above crossed cutlasses wreaked havoc across the busy shipping lanes while encountering minimal resistance.

Rackham and his men, following the successful raid and destruction of yet another Spanish merchant ship, furled their sails and retreated below decks to celebrate their good fortune. They broke open a keg of dark rum and drank themselves into a state of unconsciousness. It was the second week of October 1720.

At the first hint of dawn's purple skies, the English Captain Jonathan Barret led a boarding party onto the decks of *The William*. Only Anne Bonny and her friend Mary Reade put up a meaningful fight, taking out six of the naval invaders before surrendering. Overwhelmed by the sheer number of armed attackers, and suffering the ill effects of their drunken stupor, Rackham and his band yielded without drawing their weapons. The British put the cutthroats in leg irons, chained them together in the brig of the English frigate, and set sail for Port Royal and the court of Jamaica's sadistic Governor.

Once ashore, the pirates were crowded into small dank cells, shackled to mold-covered walls, and left to hang in a semi-standing position, saturated with their own waste. Their unsupported body weight caused ligaments and cartilage to separate painfully from the ribs and joints while their muscles burned without relief. The floggings started on the second day of their imprisonment and continued daily, until the date of sentencing. Under the direction of prison guards, inmates trying to earn clemency from the authorities, beat the crewmembers with savage enthusiasm, using cat o' nine tails, an implement made with a short wooden handle binding leather straps with sharpened bone fragments attached at the ends. The whips lashed across bare skin, cutting deep into the tissue, turning the backs of the men into bloody pulp and gore. When the trials began, Rackham and his crew longed for the relief that death would bring.

Anne Bonny and Mary Reade were not beaten or chained. Each was expecting a child and even the brutal Governor could not justify the torture and execution of women in their condition. Mary suffered with fever, which worsened each day. Anne's only chance for reprieve rested in the hands of her wealthy father in South Carolina, a man always determined to have his way. She hoped he could bribe the local officials to gain her release, but time was her greatest enemy, as word of her capture would take weeks to reach him. She was due to deliver within two months, and scheduled for execution soon thereafter. Staring toward the gallows through tear-filled eyes and the rusted bars of her cell, she trembled, overwhelmed with grief and terror as she watched the man she loved, the father of her unborn child, prepare to meet death.

A light sea breeze stirred, providing a brief respite from the searing heat. As the executioner nodded, acknowledging the order to carry out his duties, Rackham lifted his head high, taking in the sweet smell of salt air. He felt Anne's stare and, determined to die bravely, offered one last carefree smile and nod in her direction. The sand-filled bags dropped as the hatch cover fell away. Jack, still smiling, plunged a full body length through the opening. As the rope went taut, his neck snapped with a loud crack, sending an excruciating, but short-lived pain throughout his body. The last sensation was the pressure behind the eyes, relieved when his left eye exploded outward to land blindly against his cheek. For several seconds the swaying corpse twitched grotesquely from the end of the rope. Calico Jack Rackham was dead.

Seven weeks passed. Mary Reade died in early January; babbling incoherently through her miserable last days. On January 19th, Anne Bonny gave birth to a healthy son and named him Jacob Rackham. An old woman assigned to her care quietly confided that Anne would face a firing squad, not the gallows. No pardon was expected and her appointment with the executioner drew near. While she accepted it, her fears for her infant son's fate tore at her soul.

On the first day of February, they came for her. The escorts, dressed formally in their red military uniforms, allowed Anne to carry her baby as they marched in time with the beating snare drums into the courtyard in the center of the prison grounds. With her back against the wall, facing three riflemen, she kissed her son, tears soaking the baby's velvety cheeks. A woman approached and, with a sorrowful look, removed the infant from Anne's arms, and stepped away as the executioner placed a black hood over the young mother's head. Her killers stood at the ready as they read the pronouncement of her sentence aloud. Midway through the proceedings, soldiers charged through the square on horseback shouting orders to stop the execution. Payment of a substantial bribe had reached the Governor, a full pardon granted in exchange. The shrieking crowd, cheated of their entertainment, watched helplessly as the soldiers whisked Anne and her baby past the mob to the wharf and a waiting merchant ship.

The seas were calm and the winds favorable as they sailed through the straits between Cuba and Saint-Dominguez. After a three-day sail, the vessel moored in the still waters of New Providence in the Bahamas. While the ship's crew offloaded cargo, Anne gathered up little Jacob and slipped past her father's chaperones. With her face partially covered, she made her way into town.

Checking in all directions to make sure no one had followed, Anne entered a tavern. Her heart pounded as she kept her head tilted away from a handful of ragged patrons. It was a familiar place, where she and her former shipmates had gathered during better times. Sneaking into a back room and quietly latching the door behind her, she leaned against the frame, allowing herself a moment to regain her composure. Finally, Anne knelt and carefully pried open one of the floorboards. Tossing it aside, she reached below and probed through the coarse loose sand. Several agonizing minutes passed. Her search ended when she retrieved three copper discs. Anne tucked the saucer-sized plates inside the folds of the blanket wrapped around her tiny son before replacing the board. She crept to the opposite side of the room and pushed open the shutters. Balancing precariously on top of an empty rum barrel, she climbed through the small window and, staying to the less traveled side streets, hurried unnoticed back to the ship.

Sitting inside the cramped cabin aboard ship, she ran her fingers gently across the discs, all of them engraved with a curious series of lines and numerals. She smiled sadly wondering what might have been. The engravings, meaningless to anyone but Anne Bonny and Jack Rackham, pinpointed the location of a vast stockpile of stolen relics and treasures collected during their yearlong reckless endeavor.

Anne returned in disgrace to her father's plantation, never to venture beyond its boundaries again. In the last days before her death, she shared with her son stories of his father and of her own life of piracy, but the mystery of the discs remained a secret.

Jacob Rackham inherited his grandfather's lands, and enjoyed prosperity and social status well into his old age. On the fortieth anniversary of his father's execution, he erected a headstone in the family's cemetery, next to his mother's marker with the name *Calico Jack Rackham* etched into its face. The tribute would have pleased Anne Bonny.

Nearly three centuries following the death of Calico Jack Rackham, a man with a pure white goatee and pair of intense aqua blue eyes purchased three copper discs for the sum of eight dollars from a cluttered antique shop near the South Carolina coast. The buyer, a treasure hunter named Rackham, left the store with his new find clutched securely in the crook of his arm. A tiny bell jingled as the shop door closed behind him and, at that very moment, ten miles inland, a single bolt of lightning burned through the cloudless blue skies, striking the gravestone of Calico Jack, leaving behind a scorched jagged crack through its center.

RECKLESS ENDEAVOR

PRESENT DAY
SAINT AUGUSTINE, FLORIDA

～1～
TREASURY STREET

～IT WAS A MUFFLED SCREAM. Sixteen-year-old Jack Rackham walked through the deserted streets of St. Augustine toward his Jeep parked in the empty lot on the corner of Charlotte and Treasury Street. Had he walked another ten feet, he would have missed it, making the start of his summer vacation uneventful. A sobbing sound escaped from between two buildings, loud enough to make him change direction.

Careful not to give away his position, he ran toward the source of the commotion and stopped. Leaning his shoulder against a crumbling stucco covered wall, he peered around the corner into an alleyway between two houses. A fence, twenty feet from the walkway, connected the properties. Crud encrusted dumpsters were set on each side, leaving a double gate exposed at the center. The pink glare from a streetlight spilled a third of the way into the gap, but beyond, everything was gray, barely light enough for him to see two figures edging their way toward the filthy containers. One was small, probably the victim, the positioning defensive, moving backwards. The other, a man, stalking with his arm extended. Jack could hear most of the conversation. They were out of breath from fear or exertion, maybe both.

Treasury Street—Saint. Augustine, Florida

"Get in the car. I swear I'll use this." The man's voice was gravelly; he had to be older, probably a smoker, a heavy smoker.

"No. I'll scream. The cops will come." It was the panicked voice of a young female. Her voice quivered, barely audible, not much of a threat.

"You would have screamed by now. You can't afford to get caught."

"I'm not getting in any car. I'm dead if I go with you."

"You'll get in the car, I don't care how. Dead suits me fine." The man closed the gap, taking small swipes and jabs at the smaller figure, as she reached the far corner, trapped against the reeking dumpsters.

Jack stepped from behind the building, making no effort at stealth. He needed to draw attention to himself and cleared his throat as the soles of his deck shoes scraped the loose stones half-covered in grass. The startled man turned sideways, keeping himself positioned between the intruder and the girl, with the knife pointed.

"Got a problem here?" asked Jack.

"Hit the road, punk. This isn't your business." The man kept his head down, trying to conceal his features, but didn't hide the weapon.

Jack took two steps forward. "You're wrong old man. It is my business now. A girl trapped by some nut isn't something I'm going to walk away from. Use your head and let her go." His voice was calm, authoritative, and confident, but his insides were churning. This could end badly for someone, maybe everyone.

There was no turning back and all three knew it. It was two against one, but the knife evened the odds. Jack started toward the attacker, his hands held away from his body, fingers loose, waiting for the first thrust. The girl crouched next to the trash bins, clinging to the strap of a light colored bag. She had calmed a bit, as if there was some slim hope for escape. Her eyes darted between her rescuer and attacker.

The man looked desperate. He was smaller than Jack, wore thick framed glasses and his hand shook slightly as he flashed the sharp blade. His eyes flickered, searching for the opportunity to attack or escape. Jack turned, leaving the attacker an opening for escape as they faced one another from six feet apart.

"Look man, nobody needs to get hurt here. Just take off down the street and we'll forget this ever happened." Jack closed the gap to four feet, trying to force a move.

The man seemed to consider it. Jack knew the instant the man decided to strike and braced himself for the attack. The telltale was the slow lean toward the street. It was meant to be deceptive, but the motion was awkward and the pause too long, giving away the man's true intent. Jack spread his feet, in line with his broad shoulders. Prepared. Balanced. He reacted with the start of the slicing windmill motion of the knife. It was over in seconds.

Stepping to his left as the knife arced toward his chest Jack grabbed the man's wrist on the downward swing with his right hand while his left crashed hard against the man's forearm. The arm snapped and the knife clattered to the ground. Still gripping the man's wrist, Jack twisted his upper body, using the momentum of the initial lunge to swing the attacker in a counterclockwise motion, releasing the grip before the man's back and head smashed against the wall. The sound was sickening, a wet solid thud, flesh and bone colliding with thick stucco over heavy timber.

The man bounced, wobbled, and collapsed face first, unconscious, onto the driveway's mix of gravel and grass. A dark bloodstain, a heavy blotch, with dripping tentacles scattered from the center, marked the point of impact. Jack worried that the man might be dead and knelt to check. There was a pulse, the breathing shallow and labored. The man needed an ambulance, a fast one. Jack made the call from his cell.

"911 operator, what is your emergency?"

"There's an injured man here on Treasury Street. He needs EMTs now."

"What is the nature of the injury?"

"He's been knocked unconscious, still has a pulse, but is having difficulty breathing." The wail of sirens started from somewhere nearby.

"Units are on the way. Please remain on the scene to offer any possible assistance."

The County Sheriff arrived soon after the connection to the operator was broken, and just before Jack noticed the girl had disappeared. It would complicate things.

It took sixty seconds to discover how complicated, as officers positioned his hands behind his back and zipped them into a pair of flex cuffs. The beefy hand of a deputy patted him down and guided him toward a white cruiser with green striping and gold lettering spelling out *St. John's County Sheriff's Department*, this followed by firm instructions to sit in the back seat and behave. A pair of EMTs arrived with their orange equipment cases, while police barricaded the area to keep curious onlookers at bay. Jack slid across the seat as the cruiser door slammed shut. With the windows closed, and the engine shut down, the heat inside the car built to a stifling level. Left alone to sweat and worry, he stared at the red and blue lights pulsing around the crime scene.

They escorted him to a holding cell at the Sheriff's headquarters. So far, no one seemed interested in hearing his account of the incident. The cuffs dug into his wrists and his shoulders ached from having his arms pinned behind his back. Fluorescent fixtures hummed overhead. A deputy deposited his wallet, keys, cash, and cell phone in a clear plastic bag, leaving it unattended on an empty desk.

The sound of keys in the lock caused Jack to stir. Exhausted, he had dozed off with his head tucked against his shoulder leaving a painful knot in the back of his neck. An officer with a stern, no nonsense look, dressed in a crisp, tight fitting green uniform, filled the doorway, muscles bulging against the bottom of rolled up shirtsleeves, and with two fingers, motioned for the teenager to follow. The man was at least four inches taller than Jack.

The officer picked up the bag of personal effects from the desk as they crossed to a room with a plate identifying it with the single word *Interview*. The door locked following their entry and the officer removed the cuffs. Jack rubbed his wrists and rotated his arms to restore the blood flow. He had no idea what to expect as he surveyed the room. Block walls, painted a glaring shade of white surrounded a table. A microphone and recorder sat in the center while a wall mounted camera pointed at one of two chairs.

"I'm Lieutenant Marinara. I want you to tell me what went on there on Charlotte Street a few hours ago. The tape recorder and camera are off, by the way."

Jack was nervous and confused, unsure of what was expected. "Aren't you going to read me my rights or something?"

"We're not charging you with anything yet."

"Yet? Maybe I ought to get my grandfather down here with a lawyer."

"You got something to hide?"

"No sir, not at all."

"So tell me the story."

Jack thought it through for a minute, making sure he had the details straight in his mind. He looked over at the lieutenant. "Okay, but if I'm not being charged with anything *yet*, meaning I might be later, why should I tell you what happened without an attorney?"

"I can keep you locked up here all night, maybe longer."

"Seems like I've been here most of the night already. My grandparents must be worried. At least call them so they know I'm alright."

"You make the call and when you're done, I want to hear the story and I mean the whole story, nothing left out. Got it?" The officer stood and walked toward the door. It buzzed and unlocked as his hand touched the handle. So far, nothing was working the way it did on TV. He had also never seen a cop as huge as Lieutenant Marinara.

They walked to a cubicle in the middle of the room. The officer picked up the phone, pressed the number nine and handed it to Jack. "You have three minutes," he said and walked to an open door twenty feet away.

Jack couldn't explain the details to Pop in three minutes, just assured him that he had acted in self-defense. Pop wanted to talk to the Lieutenant but Marinara refused and pointed to his watch seconds before the line went dead.

Back in the interview room, it started again. "I let you make your call, now tell me what happened."

"I was walking to my Jeep and heard a scream from between two buildings. I ran toward the sound and found some nut waving a knife, and a girl backing up, trying to get away. He had her trapped next to some dumpsters. I stepped in and he came after me. When he swung at me with the knife, I grabbed his wrist, slammed my fist against his forearm and threw him against the wall. His head hit the stucco and knocked him out. The girl must have run away while I called 911."

"That's it? That's the story? You didn't hear what they were saying?"

"I heard him tell the girl to get in the car. She refused and said if she got in the car, she would be dead. He said she would be getting in the car one way or the other."

"You didn't just attack some old guy so you could rob him?"

"What?"

"You heard me. I don't stutter. You're a big kid. What are you six-three, two hundred n' ten pounds?"

"Six-four, two-twenty."

"You work out a lot? Football player?"

"I work out. Don't play football."

"Why not? A kid your size should be playing football."

"I spend every summer here with my grandparents. Back home, football camp starts at the beginning of August. I'd rather surf and hang out with my friends down here."

"Where are you from?"

"You know that already. It's on my ID."

"Answer the question."

"I'm from Camp Hill, Pennsylvania. My grandparents live near Crescent Beach. I'm sixteen, have never been in trouble and didn't go looking for any tonight."

"Did you beat the guy up to get his money?"

"No."

"How come a sixteen-year-old is running around with over four hundred dollars?"

"What's wrong with that?"

"Don't see too many sixteen-year-olds around here with that kind of cash on them. Can you prove how you got it?"

Jack paused. "I can show you an ATM receipt showing a withdrawal today."

"How long have you been in town?"

"Got here this afternoon."

"You're off to a flying start."

"Maybe next time I'll mind my own business."

"Maybe you wanted to make a few bucks off someone smaller and weaker. Make a little vacation money."

Jack's face reddened. "I don't need the money Lieutenant."

"Oh, really, why's that?"

"I'm a millionaire."

"This is getting good. You're an out-of-town sixteen-year-old millionaire. You beat someone up, put him in the hospital, and tell me he threatened someone with a knife and that makes you the hero. The man's wallet is missing and there's no victim, no witness, and no weapon at the scene. You want to run all of this by me one more time, you know, for the record?"

Jack slumped in his chair. "Why would I beat someone up, call 911, and then hang around for you guys?"

"Maybe so we would believe your story. Maybe you thought the old guy would die and then you'd face a murder charge and this was the only way to cover your tracks. Too bad there's no knife, it kind of blows a hole in your story. So, you want to try again? This time, let's start with the truth."

"I've told you everything I know. You need to find the knife and the girl. Ask the creep why he had her cornered, trying to get her into his car?"

"What kind of car was it?"

"I don't know, didn't see it."

"Now there's an invisible car?"

Jack didn't reply.

"No, I guess you wouldn't see the invisible car, while you attacked a man with an invisible knife, cornering an invisible girl. Do I have it right?"

"I'm done now. You don't believe me so I'll wait for a lawyer."

Lieutenant Marinara stood. "What if I told you I lied and taped the conversation?"

"It wouldn't matter. The story's the same, on or off tape."

"What did this girl look like?"

"I told you, I'm finished talking. I want a lawyer."

"Tell me what she looked like."

"She was crouching, backing up, trying to get away. All I could tell was she had light-colored hair and carried a tan or beige bag with a long strap. The lighting wasn't good."

"What do you remember about the man?"

"He had thick glasses with dark frames, and wore a ratty looking golf hat, the kind with a brim all the way around. I'd say he was maybe six feet tall and thin. He had gray shaggy hair sticking out from under the hat."

"How come you can describe the man but not the girl?"

Jack let out a frustrated sigh. "I could see the guy, we were face to face. I was at least fifteen feet from the girl and she was hiding in the shadows."

Officer Marinara drummed his fingers on the table. For the first time Jack noticed a tired look, something in the blood-shot eyes. "Mind if I call you Jack?"

"Do you mind if I call you Muscles?"

"What?"

"Word association, helps me remember. Muscles Marinara. Like the seafood, just not spelled the same."

Marinara smiled, almost chuckled. "Let's stick with Lieu-tenant."

"So is this where you turn up the heat trying to make me slip up and contradict some part of my story?"

Lieutenant Marinara ignored the remark. "The guy you sent to the hospital is one of the wealthiest business owners in the entire county."

Jack leaned forward placing his chin in the palm of his left hand, a look of resignation on his face. "So that means what to me? The kid from out of town assaulted a fine, upstanding citizen, without a trace of provocation."

"Provocation? That's a big word for a kid your age."

"I'm smarter than I look."

"We need to find the knife."

Jack looked at the Lieutenant. "Sounds like you might believe me."

"I really want to, Jack."

⌒2⌒
HOMELESS AND HUNGRY

⌒THE GIRL WATCHED THEM ESCORT the big kid into the sheriff's office. She knew they would bring him here when she saw them putting him in cuffs, while she cowered behind a line of shrubs. Taking the knife had been a big mistake. It was the evidence the kid needed to prove his innocence.

A black Escalade pulled up in front of the station, and parked in a tow away zone. An older man jumped from the SUV and rushed into the building. She suspected he had something to do with the kid. It was time to try to make things right.

Hugging the shadows, she ran across the lot to the Escalade, hoping to find it unlocked. It was. She climbed into the driver's side, bent down, hidden below the dashboard and fumbled through her canvas bag collecting the knife and wallet. It would provide enough proof to make them let the kid go. Returning the money hurt, but she probably owed him her life, so she left the wallet intact and placed it, with the knife, on the console. That done, she ran as fast as she could from the parking lot, away from the glaring lights that could give her away.

The foul mood was obvious when Jack's grandfather demanded to see the officer in charge. A tired looking Lieutenant Marinara walked into the waiting area, a cup of coffee in each hand. Pop didn't exchange pleasantries.

"What's goin' on here, Sergeant?"

"It's Lieutenant Marinara, sir and you must be … Mr. Rackham."

"That's correct an' I intend to get him outta this jailhouse right now, Corporal."

"It's Lieutenant, and I'm hoping to get him out of here as well, before you demote me again." Officer Marinara knew he was up against a feisty character, one not easily intimidated.

"Is he under arrest?"

"No he's not."

"Then why you holdin' him?"

"He may have some information that could prove helpful in an investigation. I happen to believe his story but there's some important evidence missing that would help clear things up."

"I'll repeat my question, sir. If he's not under arrest and if you *think* he's tellin' the truth, why is he still here at nearly three in the morning?" Pop was relentless when he wanted his way.

Lieutenant Marinara handed Pop the coffee. "Let's start over. I grilled Jack thoroughly. He put a guy in the hospital. Claims the man attacked him with a knife."

"So if that's what he said, that's what happened. That boy doesn't lie."

"We can't find the knife and we found more than four hundred dollars in Jack's pocket."

"So go look for the knife. I'll bet if it was under a jelly doughnut you'd find it. He didn't rob anybody if that's what you're thinkin'. Wouldn't have to, he's a millionaire."

Marinara rubbed his eyes and sighed. "Sir, first of all, look at me. Do you really think I eat jelly doughnuts?"

"How would I know? Some people have high metabolisms, can eat anything n' don't gain a pound. Not me, junk like that goes right to my gut."

"OK, let's assume the knife's not under a doughnut, I'll even concede that Jack is a millionaire…"

"He is a millionaire. I can prove that easy enough. The kid hit it big treasure huntin' last year. Every nickel is legit too."

"You're serious."

"You think I'm in the mood to joke around at this hour?"

"So why would he break a guy's arm and slam him into a brick wall?"

"Because the guy had a knife. Didn't you listen to his story? I got it first time through."

"What makes a sixteen-year-old kid take on a guy with a knife to rescue a girl?"

"Didn't hear about the girl," said Pop.

"Supposedly, he heard a scream and found a man threatening a girl with a knife. It happened over at Treasury and Charlotte Street. The knife, the man's wallet, and the girl were not accounted for when we arrived on the scene," explained Marinara.

"So what's the problem? He rescues the girl, she runs off with the knife n' wallet, somebody hears the commotion and calls the cops. There, took me three seconds to figure all of that out. Now let him loose so we can get outta here n' you can go find the girl."

"It doesn't work that way, sir. Without the girl and the knife, it's just his version of the story. I'm still curious. Why would a sixteen-year-old take that kind of risk?"

"He look like a wimp to you?"

"No, but the guy had a knife."

"No grandson of mine would let somethin' happen to a woman without steppin' up in her defense. That boy's tough, and he's a good kid. It's the way he was raised. So, this person that called 911, what did they report?"

"Jack called 911."

"Oh, well that makes even more sense. My grandson, the *mugger,* calls the cops and then hangs out to get himself arrested."

"Sir, here's the situation. Jack probably interrupted an attempted abduction. We've had three attacks on young women in the last four months. Maybe it's related. Maybe it's not. That information, by the way, has to be kept quiet. We don't need a panic on our hands. Now, for what it's worth, I believe Jack's telling the truth."

"Who was the guy with the knife?"

"I can't tell you that," said Marinara.

"So what's that mean? Jack stays in jail 'til you find the knife or the girl?"

"No, I'm working on a way around that. Maybe I could release him into your custody with the understanding that he won't leave town."

"So I'm a warden now."

"That's not what I meant."

"Do you think he's innocent or not?"

"Yes sir, I do."

"Then let him out. He'll cooperate and answer any questions you have."

"He's been very cooperative, Mr. Rackham."

"See that, Corporal? He's got nothin' to hide. I'll give you my address and phone number in case anything comes up. If you want to stop by for a chat, call ahead and we'll be more than happy to do whatever we can to help. We'll be in town for about two weeks and then, we're takin' a boat trip to the islands."

"Alright, let me take care of some paperwork, and get him on his way before I get demoted one more time. I have one more question. You're not jerkin' my chain about the millionaire thing, are you?"

"Whaddya mean the millionaire thing? Me or Jack?"

"Who's the millionaire? Is it his money or yours?"

"We're both millionaires. Both of us made big bucks in the treasure huntin' game, separate finds. His money is his and mine is mine. The way it should be."

The Lieutenant shook his head and walked out of the room. Fifteen minutes later, they released Jack into Pop's custody.

"This is one of the more unusual starts to your summertime visit," said Pop as they walked down the steps toward the Escalade.

"I'm sorry about the trouble, but I had to do something," answered Jack.

"No problem. I'd come unglued if my grandson ignored someone in trouble."

"We've got to find that girl. I think the Lieutenant believes me, but that's not going to make my problem disappear. There's nothing to back up my story about the knife and if the old guy finds out there's no proof against him, he's going to make my life miserable," said Jack as they reached the shiny black SUV.

"You're right on all counts Jackson, but you didn't actually see the girl, so how can we find her?" Pop climbed into the driver's seat and reached for the ignition. The keys were missing and he searched his pockets.

"I know I didn't take my keys inside."

"You left the lights on too. What's up with that? Gettin' senile all of a sudden?"

Pop shook his head. "Senile? You wanna walk home? Guess I wasn't thinkin' straight. Maybe I did take 'em with me and left 'em inside. Sit tight a minute." He opened the door to return to the station and the interior overhead light blinked on.

Jack noticed the keys sitting on the console. They were lying on top of a wallet and a knife. Someone wanted them found. The door slammed before he could get Pop's attention. As Pop walked past the front grill of the SUV, Jack stretched across to tap the horn. He lost his balance, enough to make him lean heavily against the steering wheel. The horn blared in a loud sustained blast causing Pop to jump straight into the air.

"Whaddya doin', tryin' to give me heart failure?" Pop yelled as he yanked open the passenger side door. Jack shoved one hand across his mouth to stifle a laugh and hide the expanding grin on his face. With his free hand, he pointed toward the console, half-expecting Pop to drag him by the collar from the Escalade and onto the pavement to face a wagging index finger.

Pop spotted the keys resting on top of the wallet and knife. "It looks like we had a visit from a concerned citizen."

"It must have been the girl," said Jack. "If so, she's got to be close by, probably watching to make sure we found the stuff."

Pop nodded in agreement. "My guess is she's across the street. I'll run this inside, you see if you can track her down. She's probably runnin' by now, so she's got at least a ninety-second head start. You'd better sprint."

Jack bolted toward a row of buildings across the lot while Pop used a black kerchief to gather the knife and wallet without transferring his own fingerprints. He walked toward the double doors leading to the police station, where he intercepted Lieutenant Marinara at the top of the stairs.

"Mr. Rackham. I thought you'd be long gone by now."

"Yeah, me too, but someone left us a present while we were inside. This was on my car's console," said Pop as he handed the bundle over.

"It seems someone wanted to make sure your grandson didn't get the blame after doing his good deed."

"I toldja he was tellin' the truth."

"If I didn't believe him, he'd be in a cell right now. Look. I'm not the bad guy, Mr. Rackham, just doing my job."

Pop turned and pointed across the street. "Lieutenant, I appreciate your position. We'll do everything we can to help you get the answers you're lookin' for. In fact, Jack is runnin' around now, tryin' to find the girl. Whaddya think she's runnin' from?

Lieutenant Marinara ignored the question, pressed the button on a shoulder-mounted microphone and ordered a pair of squad cars to search the area for a teenage girl carrying a light-colored canvas bag.

Jack spotted her three blocks from the county complex and slowed to a half-jog. She walked fast, without looking around, so he kept his distance to see where she was going. He followed her into the center of town where she ducked into an alleyway behind a popular restaurant. Keeping her in sight, he watched as she helped herself to water from an outside spigot. Once finished drinking and washing her face, the girl rummaged through the trashcans near the back door before sitting in the shadows to eat a handful of scraps. Jack moved from his hiding place, his hands held up in an *all is okay* gesture. The girl jumped to her feet, dropping her food in the process, but said nothing.

He sat on one of the cans ten feet away. "Want to tell me what's going on?"

She offered no reply, simply shook her head no. Through the shadows, it was impossible to make out her features. The bulky clothes didn't hide the fact that she was slightly built and on the tall side, maybe five feet six or seven.

"Thanks for leaving that wallet and knife for me. I was having a hard time proving that I didn't attack the guy for his money."

Still, she offered no response.

From the corner of his eye, Jack spotted a police cruiser driving toward the alley. "We need to hide. The police are looking for you and there's a car moving this way from Hypolita Street." He stood and moved to the side of the restaurant behind a pair of propane tanks. He was joined a moment later by the girl, only seconds before the beam of the cruiser's spot-light crawled across the back wall of the building.

As the patrol car continued past, Jack reached into his pocket, removed his cell phone, punched in a number and waited. It took two attempts to get beyond voicemail before he finally spoke. "Kai. It's me. Yeah, I know it's late but I need a favor. Yeah, I got to town late this afternoon. Ran into a little problem that's all... You said that already. Pick me up at Cordova Street so I can get my Jeep. Okay. I'll explain everything later. Right. Thanks. See you in a few."

He turned toward the girl. "My name's Jack Rackham. I'll do what I can to help, but you've got to trust me. Okay?"

"Sorry, I don't trust anyone. No offense, but it's better if I get going. I've caused you enough trouble. Thanks for everything, but it's gotta be this way." She reached for her bag.

"That's it?"

"Guess so."

"You'd rather keep scrounging meals from garbage cans?"

"I've only done that a couple of times."

"Tell you what; let's get you off the street for the night. Come back to the house with me and meet my grandparents. If nothing else, you'll be able to get some decent food and rest before going on your way."

"Are you nuts? I don't know you. You could be a creep like that old man."

"You know that's not true. What's your name?"

"Rachel. Rachel Lane."

"Okay, Rachel Lane, that's a start. What do you need most? Food? Money? Clothes? I can get you food and money now. You're out of luck on the clothes 'til the stores open…"

"Why would you…?"

"I don't know. Looks like you could use some help that's all. You want to stay here all alone and take your chances? That's up to you. I'm not going to beg. My friend will be here in a few minutes to give me a lift. I asked him to do that so the police wouldn't see the two of us walking through town. They're looking for you, not me. Frankly, I don't need the aggravation." Jack shoved both hands in his pockets before edging his way toward the street looking north, where he waited, watching for Kai's yellow Jeep to make the turn. When he saw headlights, he pulled out a handful of folded bills and reached out, offering them to Rachel. "Here, it's yours," he said.

Rachel hesitated. She needed money desperately and had lied about the number of times she had scrounged meals from restaurant trashcans. The kid had stuck his neck out already, and now offered her a chance to get off the street for the night. The past few months had taught her that some risks were worth taking. Reluctantly, she walked over to stand beside him, and, for the first time, noticed Jack was huge. Certainly, he could have hurt her if he had wanted to. Her empty stomach rumbled as she reached his side.

"That looks like a lot of money, Jack."

"It's about four hundred and fifty bucks. Go ahead. Take it."

"If it's okay with you, I'd rather go to your grandparent's house. You asked me to trust you. I don't know what else to do, so I hope I'm not making a mistake."

Jack nodded and put the cash away as Kai's Jeep pulled alongside. "It's okay. My grandparents will have a gazillion questions, but they're great people. You'll be safe."

Rachel relaxed. The barest trace of a smile appeared as she clutched the straps of her bag and climbed into the Jeep.

"So, Rackham, you wanna explain why I'm playin' cab driver at this hour? Who's this?"

"Kai, this is Rachel. Rachel, meet Kai."

"Hi, Rachel. You're not too picky 'bout who you hang out with."

Jack rolled his eyes. "Rachel ran into a problem, a simple misunderstanding, so she's going back to the house until things settle down."

"Simple misunderstanding? Is that why the cops are all drivin' around shinin' spotlights in backyards and alleys?" Kai stared toward Rachel through the rearview mirror.

"Are they really?" she asked.

"Yup. They shined their lights at me when I drove by. Wanna tell me what's goin' on?"

Jack explained only the most important details while Kai drove toward the parking lot. A deputy was sitting in a Ford Explorer scoping out Jack's red Jeep Wrangler parked under the gloom of a light pole.

"Drop me here and take Rachel to the house. Wait in the driveway." He didn't hang around for an answer and exited to the street before Kai could come to a complete stop. Jack stuffed his hands in his pockets and walked nonchalantly toward his own Jeep as Kai drove off.

Kai and Rachel pulled up to the entrance of the Rackham estate next to a security pedestal with a polished brass keypad standing at the left hand side of the driveway. After tapping out a series of numbers, a green light flickered and the massive ornamental iron gates swung inward. They rode through the shrub and palm-lined lane toward the back of the house.

Rachel stared ahead. "This is where Jack lives?"

"Only during the summer. This place belongs to his grandparents."

"No wonder he had so much money in his pocket."

Kai glanced her way as she took in the surroundings. "What do you know about him?"

"Nothing. He helped me out of…a bad situation. We didn't have much of a chance to talk. I wasn't going to come here when he first offered but, for some reason, I felt like I could trust him and I needed to get off the street." Signs of strain and exhaustion were showing and she sighed as she explained, while trying not to cry.

Kai parked in front of the garage, and leaned back with his hands clasped behind his head. "He's a good guy. I'd trust him with my life. Actually, I've already done that a few times. It sucked, but I'm still here. I was gonna ask why you robbed the old man, but the real question is, why are you on your own? You can tell me it's none of my business if you want."

"I don't have anyone. My father passed away when I was little and my mom died this past Christmas Eve. After the funeral, I lived in a miserable foster home; actually, it was more like a prison. I think the people took in kids to make extra money. While they were out picking up another kid, I grabbed my stuff and broke out through a basement window. Then I walked into town, emptied my savings account, and jumped a bus to Florida. I figured, better to be homeless where it was warm. My money finally ran out a few weeks ago. That's when I learned to pick pockets."

"Why didn't you try to get some kind of job?"

"You're the real sympathetic type."

"I am. I just don't understand why you didn't try to work instead of bein' a crook."

Rachel looked at Kai, unsure whether to be embarrassed or angry. "I've had several jobs. No one will hire me full-time because of my age and I can't earn enough part-time to afford a place to live. With no address, the only work I can get is washing dishes, usually in exchange for a few bucks and a meal. I'm not lazy and don't want to steal or become a charity case."

"So robbin' the old guy was just a way to survive."

"No. Well, yes, partly. The guy was a creep. He made some disgusting remarks to me earlier when I was resting on a bench. Mostly I needed the money but I wanted to get even for … for what he said. I followed him for about an hour. He went into a bookstore, and when he was reading the back cover of a book, I picked his pocket. My mistake was turning around for one last look as I went through the door. He recognized me, checked his pocket and chased me. I made a wrong turn and he cornered me in an alley, the one where Jack found us." The tears started to flow and she bit her lip to stifle a sob.

Jack pulled up in the driveway and parked next to Kai. It was past five in the morning.

~3~
THE RACKHAMS

RACHEL SAT IN THE SCREENED-IN lanai between Pop and Nan, sipping on a tall glass of orange juice. She had finished a hot breakfast of pancakes, scrambled eggs and bacon while listening to the calm and patient conversation about the events of the previous night.

Nan noticed Rachel's struggle to stay awake and placed a hand on her arm. "Let me show you to one of the guest rooms so you can get some rest. There will be plenty of time to talk later."

She followed Nan into the house, walking across gleaming white marble floors, taking in the lavish décor of the grand house. It was like nothing she had seen in her life. The guest room was as big as the apartment that Rachel had shared with her mom. Nan spread a white nightgown and terry robe over the end of the bed.

"Through that door next to the closet you'll find your own bathroom. Make yourself at home and get some sleep. Everything will be fine. We'll chat after you wake up," said Nan.

"Thank you, Mrs. Rackham. I promise not to mess anything up."

"Don't be silly, and please, call me Nan. A hot shower and a nice firm bed and you'll feel like a new woman."

The Rackham Estate

Rachel showered, changed and fell asleep within ten minutes, her cares temporarily forgotten. She had never slept in such a huge bed.

X

Nan returned to the porch and took her seat at the table. "What are we going to do? She has nowhere to go. We need to help her or she'll end up being cared for by some agency again."

Pop didn't hesitate. "I'm gonna go see that Lieutenant. He's got the old man's knife now so it's unlikely the old creep will press charges. The guy's gonna have a tough time explainin' why he had the kid cornered like that, even if she did steal his wallet. If we act as temporary guardians, assumin' Rachel is agreeable, she can stay with us 'til she decides what she wants to do. She's a long way from what used to be home. I looked it up. Auburn Maine is about fourteen hundred miles north of here."

"What about the trip?" asked Jack. "Would she go with us?"

Pop squeezed the bridge of his nose and squinted. "Hadn't thought about that. The new boat will be here in a few days. It was in Hatteras yesterday. Well, I guess we'll cross that bridge later. First we need to get Rachel taken care of." He stood, gave Nan a peck on the cheek and walked to the garage.

Nan turned toward Jack. "He's been all amped up about that boat and the trip. I call it his overpriced dingy just to get on his nerves. Go get some rest while your grandfather gets this dilemma solved."

"Do you think he can fix this?" asked Jack through a yawn.

"Now what do you think? Have you ever known him not to get his way?"

"Guess you're right, Nan. Let's hope he keeps his streak alive. Watching her eat garbage from that…it's the saddest thing I think I've ever seen, at least in person."

"I agree. It's heartbreaking. Please, go get some sleep. Dream about our island cruise on Pop's new floating money pit," said Nan as Jack stood to leave.

Pop had purchased *Reckless Endeavor,* a one hundred twenty-two-foot schooner, the previous summer. For ten months, the hundred-year-old boat had been dry-docked in Rhode Island while a master boat builder installed new engines, rigging, and state-of-the-art electronics before restoring the exterior to its original appearance in every detail. Pop expected the massive sailboat to look authentic while performing to modern standards. He had a lead on another hidden treasure and planned to spend part of the summer searching for it in the Bahamas with Jack.

Jack climbed the stairs to a spacious apartment above the boathouse. Nan and Pop always let him use it whenever he visited. As usual, his grandparents had everything set up with anything he could want. After a quick shower, he collapsed onto the bed just as the hammering at the door started. With a groan, he crawled from the bed and shuffled to the door to find Kai and Val leaning against the railing.

"Hey guys. How are you, Val? Come on in." Jack greeted Val with a playful hug as she entered the room.

"Whaddya doin'? Who said you two could get all huggin' n' stuff?" teased Kai.

Val laughed. "What's the matter, jealous?"

"Nah. Nothin' to worry about. He's already got a new girl," said Kai.

"Don't start that crap," said Jack.

"So where's Talia?" asked Kai.

"She's on vacation with her parents in California."

Val smiled. "Is your *new* girl pretty?"

"She's not my *new* girl. I guess she's okay looking. I mean, she was a mess from being, you know, homeless."

"What color eyes does she have?" asked Val.

"I have no idea. You'll get a chance to meet her later and you can see for yourself."

Val refused to back off. "Does Talia know about her yet?"

"I talked to the girl for the first time in my life three hours ago. Why the questions?" he snapped.

Kai laughed. "Relax, she wanted to make you squirm."

"Thanks. I've been up all night; most of it spent in a police station and you're playing games. Nice way to kick things off."

"Do you feel like surfin'?" asked Kai. "The waves are supposed to be pretty good in a couple of hours."

"I'm so tired right now my eyes are crossed. We can get together tonight if you want."

"Would you bring Rachel?" asked Val.

"Geez, give me a break."

"I want to meet her. See if she'll hang out with us."

"If she wants to, it's okay with me. Pop has to get some things straightened out with the Sheriff's Department first. She might be in deep trouble, besides having no family and no home. Pop and Nan want her to stay with us."

"What about the trip to the islands?" asked Kai. "Would she go with us?"

"Kai, I don't have a clue. For all I know the Sheriff or Social Services could roll in here and pick her up at any minute. It all depends on how Pop makes out and what Rachel decides. She might want to go back to Maine." Jack's eyelids were getting heavier.

Val spoke up again. "I think it's awesome what you did last night and it's cool that Pop and Nan are trying to help. We've gotta get going, so call me or Kai when you wake up. Glad you're back, Jack."

"Glad to be back. Now get outta here so I can get some sleep.

Pop explained Rachel's situation to Lieutenant Marinara.

"Mr. Rackham, I'll check the story out. I still need to tie up the loose ends with Mister W..., the man your grandson had the altercation with," said Marinara.

"What's the big secret about this guy's name? He threatened Rachel with a knife."

"She robbed the man..."

"Maybe he should've kept his filthy mouth shut. She was mindin' her own business, sittin' on a bench," argued Pop.

"That doesn't give her a free pass on this."

"I'm not sayin' she doesn't share some blame, but you can tell your buddy that if he wants to press charges, he's in for an embarrassin' battle with my attorneys. I'll get his name in time for that showdown."

"First of all, he's not my buddy. His name is Harry Wort."

"Huh?"

"The man's name is Harry Wort and he's one of the wealthiest, and most miserable, men in the county."

"With a name like Hairy Wart, no wonder he's miserable. Where'd he get a name like that?" laughed Pop.

Marinara shook his head. "It's W-O-R-T. He was named after his father,"

"So the old man's old man had a sick sense of humor."

"Look, Mr. Rackham, if you could give me a few hours, I'll speak with Social Services and see if the girl can stay with you and your wife, at least temporarily. Mr. Wort will hear of your intent to have Rachel bring charges against him for assault if he presses any against her for theft. I understand the hospital released him so I'll go over to his place myself. I'll call to let you know how it goes."

"Very good, Lieutenant, I appreciate your help and hope we can wrap this up today." The men stood and shook hands.

It was nearly five o'clock when Jack climbed out of bed and walked to the main house. He found Nan on the phone talking with Pop. She smiled at him as he sat down at the kitchen table and gave him the *thumbs up* signal. A few minutes later, she clicked the end button.

"Well, your grandfather seems to have gotten things in order. No charges are being filed and they're doing the paperwork now to give Rachel permission to stay with us. She just needs to confirm that she's agreeable to the arrangements."

"That's good news. Does Rachel know?"

"Not yet. She's still asleep. I don't know if I should just leave her alone or wake her. What do you think?" asked Nan.

"I'd say let her sleep."

"Maybe you're right. Would you mind picking up dinner for us? Pop said he'll be home shortly and I don't feel like cooking. Get enough for the four of us. I ran out earlier and bought her some clothes; hopefully I've guessed the sizes."

"What do you feel like for dinner?" asked Jack.

"Oh, I don't care. Go see Tony down at South Beach Grill. He'll get us fixed up with something delicious. Here, let me give you some money."

"I've got it, Nan." Jack spied a collection of large bags and boxes sitting on a sofa in the adjoining great room. "Did you buy out the whole store?"

Nan laughed. "That's just a warm up. When Rachel feels up to it, I'm going to teach her all about power shopping."

Jack shook his head as he walked through the back door.

Pop's tires squealed as he pulled into the garage. He had barely given the garage door opener time to do its job and narrowly missed scraping the truck's roof. A few seconds later, he stood in the kitchen next to Nan.

"One of these days you're going to drive through the back wall of that garage," said Nan.

"I have incredible skills behind the wheel, Sweets. Never gonna happen"

"Whatever. I sent Jack to pick up something for dinner."

"Good, I'm starvin'. Looks like you've been busy judgin' by that pile of bags and boxes in the other room. Didja buy out the whole store?"

"You sound like your grandson. He asked the very same question."

"Smart kid. I must've taught him right. Bein' frugal's not a crime by the way."

"You're right, Hon. Four million dollars for an oversized sailboat falls into what category?"

"It's an investment. Besides, it wasn't four million, it was three million eight. Where's Jack with that grub?" Pop knew when to change the subject. "On second thought, I'm gonna go take a nap. Didn't get hardly any sleep last night."

X

Two hours later, Pop wandered downstairs to find Nan and Rachel sitting in the great room. "I suppose you ladies are busy planning a shopping excursion," he said with a smile.

"Too late. Already set that up. Most of the stuff I picked out fits her perfectly. We were talking about some of the decisions Rachel needs to make. I explained that you were able to make the problem with that awful old man go away," said Nan.

"Good, so everything's figured out."

Rachel spoke up. "I appreciate your help, Mr. Rackham. Nan says you got permission for me to stay here while Social Services figures out what to do."

"First of all, no need for formalities with me. If you can call Mrs. Rackham Nan, you can call me Pop. Deal?"

"Deal."

"We have ninety days to work with so long as you're agreeable. The invitation for you to stay with us is wide open and we're happy to have you," said Pop.

"I feel like I'm in some kind of dream staying in this place. You've all been so nice. I'd like to stay if that's okay."

"Like I said, it's already approved. You'll have to go to the county building with me n' Nan tomorrow for an interview. They need to verify that you want to stay with us. If you say yes, they'll make us your temporary guardians. Unless you change your mind, this'll be your home for awhile." Pop paused and then frowned. "I just thought of somethin' that might make this sticky after all. Do you like boats?"

"Boats?"

"Those things that float in water. Boats."

Rachel looked toward Nan puzzled. "I'm not sure what…"

Nan interrupted. "Don't pay him any mind, he's talking in riddles. We're going to sail to the islands in a couple of weeks. We'll probably be gone for about a month."

"Maybe longer," said Pop. "So you okay doin' some sailin'?"

"I guess so. My mom took me on the ferry from Portland, Maine to Nova Scotia once when I was about seven."

"That hardly makes you a sailor but it's a start. Jack's gonna be runnin' around in his boat for sure, so ride with him as much as you can. He can help you get your sea legs. Where is that kid by the way?" asked Pop.

"He's with Kai. They went to the lighthouse," said Nan.

Pop shook his head. "The lighthouse at night? Again? After that business last year? Whatever. My stomach's growlin'. What do we have around this joint for dinner? I'm starvin'."

Nan rolled her eyes. "Jack brought stuff back from South Beach Grill while you were asleep. Can you nuke it without burning it to a crisp or blowing up the house? Rachel, let's go outside. You can check out Pop's version of the *Rackham Navy* while we're out there," she said as she stood from the sofa.

Pop grumbled as he poked buttons with labels that, to him, made no sense. Beyond making coffee, he was lost in the kitchen. *"What's this express power stuff mean anyway? Hmmm…here we go, guess it goes for, let's see, I'll try twenty minutes. Where's the clock thing? Now what? Okay, hit start. "Awww, I'm not doin' this. I'll grab dinner out,"* he muttered as he waved his hand in a *go away* gesture toward the microwave. He snatched his hat and walked out as the microwave kicked on and the carousel turned. It would be a nasty mess.

Jack and Kai sat in the park across from the lighthouse as darkness fell.

"Think Rachel's gonna stay?"

"I don't see why she wouldn't. It's not like she's got lots of options," answered Jack.

"Talia's gonna be mad if she does."

"Why?"

"Uh, maybe 'cause Rachel's really hot you dimwit. Don't go actin' like you didn't notice. Soon as Val sees her, she's gonna report to Talia."

"So let her. Talia's the one that changed all the plans around and decided to visit her friends in California instead. Now she expects us to sail all the way back to St. Augustine to pick her up. I didn't even mention *that* screwy idea to Pop."

Kai laughed. "He'd say, send 'er a post card, Jackman."

"You've got that right."

"So what're you gonna do?"

"About what?"

"Talia! You havin' trouble followin' the conversation here or somethin'?"

Jack leaned back with his arms stretched out. "It's complicated."

"What's complicated? You guys gonna break up?"

"Maybe. She's been…I don't know…drivin' me nuts lately. I was kinda glad when she went out west. I'm getting a break and she's getting her *space*," said Jack.

"Val told me awhile back that Talia's been actin' weird. Said they haven't talked much for the last coupla months and when they do, Talia's always in a rush to get off the phone," said Kai.

"Since April, maybe even March, she's been kinda out there. I don't know what her deal is, but I'm not letting her ruin my summer."

"It's probably the trip. After all the stuff that happened last summer, maybe she afraid we're gonna be doin' somethin' nuts again," replied Kai.

"What's nuts about sailing to the islands?"

"Normal people go sailing. This is a Rackham trip. We'll be lookin' for treasure on some remote island infested with cannibals. I'll betcha that's it. She decided she couldn't handle another summer of our crap." Kai folded his arms across his chest, ready to argue.

"Maybe you're right."

"Huh?"

"I said maybe you're right. Maybe she's scared. I told her a long time ago that I'm a risk taker. She knows creepy stuff doesn't bother me. Guess adventure's not so cool anymore."

"It's the cannibals. That's what did it. Scared 'er off," said Kai.

"There's no such thing as cannibals you moron."

Kai stood and looked around. "We'll see soon enough."

Jack smiled. "You got taller since last summer. Finally made it to six feet?"

"Yep. Six feet on the nose. Thought I might catch up to you but guess that ain't happenin'. Let's run over to Starbucks before they close."

Rachel and Nan paused at the dock alongside the boathouse to look at the collection of boats and jet skis, all hanging from hydraulic lifts. *Laffin' Gaff*, a thirty-eight foot Donzi with triple engines occupied the outermost lift. Closest to the walkway was *Bad Latitude*, a twenty-two foot Cobia center console with a bright blue T-Top and polished stainless steel accessories. Suspended between the two was a customized Hurricane deck boat next to a pair of two-seater jet skis. Everything glistened under the security lights.

"Is that the boat we would use to sail to the islands?" asked Rachel pointing toward the biggest boat with decals spelling out the name *Laffin' Gaff*.

"No that's what Pop calls his fishing machine. It's the one he uses to bring home the rare flounder or grouper. He's probably the worst fisherman in St. Johns County. Maybe the worst in all of Florida," said Nan.

"They don't look like, you know, the kind you could stay on for a few weeks. Where would everyone sleep?"

"We're not sailing on any of these. The new boat is much bigger. You'll see *Reckless Endeavor,* that's our sailboat, in the next few days. This one on the end, *Bad Latitude,* is Jack's boat. We're taking it with us so we can get inside little coves and shallow lagoons."

"Jack has his own boat?"

"Yes. It was a gift from an overindulgent grandfather."

"He drives it all by himself?"

"Sure. He's probably as good at handling a boat as Pop."

"How far out in the ocean will we be going?" asked Rachel.

"You would have to ask Pop or Jack. The two of them have been like kids waiting for Santa. Almost every day, since last summer, they've been back and forth on the computer or phone, working on plans and charting their course."

"I don't want to sound rude, but how did you guys… I mean, this place is incredible. The house, exotic gardens, pool, fountains, boathouse, and all of these boats, it's like…a fantasyland…"

Nan interrupted. "You want to know how we got to be wealthy."

"Well…yeah," answered Rachel, embarrassed.

"Treasure hunting. Mr. Rackham, I mean Pop, has always been fascinated by history, pirates and lost treasure. He turned his hobby into a part time job, tracked through old journals and maps, and uncovered a hidden fortune in ancient gold pieces and artifacts. After three successful expeditions, he sort of retired and then built this house. These days he coaches Jack along, teaching him what he calls the family trade."

"Jack's a treasure hunter too?"

"I suppose that would be a fair statement," said Nan, trying to suppress a smile.

"Has he found anything yet?"

"Yes, but nothing quite as valuable as what Pop has salvaged. You should ask Jack about it some time. Maybe you can get him to tell the story of his famous ancestor, a nasty pirate named Calico Jack Rackham. It's a fascinating tale. Ready to go inside? I need to see how the old geezer's dinner turned out. He's pretty lousy in the kitchen."

4
WHITE SAND AND BLUE WATER

RACHEL WATCHED JACK FROM THE kitchen window as he carried a surfboard from the garage to his bright red jeep. He was shirtless and when he lifted the board onto the overhead roll bars the muscles of his shoulders and upper arms flexed. Nan walked in and caught her staring. "He's a handsome kid, don't you think?"

Rachel felt her face burn hot with embarrassment. "Uh… yeah. I guess so."

"Are you going surfing with Jack and his friends?"

"No, I don't know how to surf."

"I'm sure you could learn."

"I don't want to intrude."

"He didn't invite you? Is that it?"

"No, but I haven't seen him since yesterday. He was gone when I woke up."

"Why don't you run upstairs and get changed. I'll see what's going on. I'm sure he won't mind taking you along. You'll get to meet Val, that's Kai's girlfriend. She's lots of fun."

"I don't know…"

"Are you worried that you're not welcome or worried about surfing?"

"Both."

Rachel Lane

"Okay. Stay here by the window and watch. I'll ask Jack if you can go. If he slumps his shoulders, that means he would rather go alone. Fair enough?"

Rachel smiled. "Sounds fair, but I have a feeling I'm being set up."

"Not at all. I want you to be comfortable. You'll have to get to know these kids sooner or later," said Nan as she walked through the back door.

Rachel kept her eyes on Jack looking for any sign that he didn't want her company. There was none. Nan said something and Jack smiled. She wasn't much of a lip reader, but thought he'd said 'sure'. When Nan turned toward window, she was smiling and Rachel ran upstairs to get changed.

Nan was waiting at the back door with a towel folded over her arm. "That wasn't so tough was it?"

Rachel was beaming. "I've never been in the ocean."

"You do know how to swim."

"Sure. You don't think Jack pretended to be nice because, you know…"

"He's always nice. Gets his disposition from me."

Jack sat behind the wheel of his Jeep with one foot propped against the side mirror. He had taken the doors off and strapped a second surfboard overhead. He greeted Rachel with a bright smile as she jumped into the passenger's seat. "Ready to rip some waves?" he asked.

"I'll give it a try. You're sure you don't mind me tagging along?"

He started the engine as she pulled on her seatbelt. "Don't mind at all. I should have asked you in the first place. Do you like country music?"

"Not especially."

"You will by the end of the summer." He laughed as he leaned forward and cranked the volume up. Jason Aldean's song My Kind Of Party blared as they turned onto A1A. When the song ended, Jack turned off the sound. After making a left hand turn, he drove less than one hundred yards, between the dunes onto a roadway leading to the beach.

"You're gonna drive down there?" asked Rachel.

Jack switched to four-wheel-drive as the front tires hit the white sand. "I always drive on the beach. That sticker on the windshield is my permit. No permit, it's six bucks."

"Look at the ocean! I've never seen it that color before. It's…it's jade green!"

"Same as your eyes." Jack groaned as the words slipped out.

"What?"

"I said what a surprise!"

"No you didn't."

"Okay then, what did I say?"

Rachel was too embarrassed to reply. He had noticed the color of her eyes. That was fair. She already knew that his were deep blue and with his long blonde hair, and tan, muscular build, he was a great looking guy, but it was his kindness and pleasant nature that she found most attractive.

Kai's yellow Jeep sat parked at the bottom edge of a dune. His bleached curly hair, often mistaken for dreads, blew in the breeze. A girl with a deep tan, wearing a bright pink bikini, stood at his side, pulling her light brown hair into a ponytail. Jack pulled alongside and switched off the engine.

"Picked up a hitchhiker?" asked Kai.

Val didn't wait to be introduced. "Hi, Rachel, I'm Val."

"Hi, Val." Rachel felt awkward, not sure what to say.

"We're gonna teach this Yankee how to surf. Think you guys are up to it?" asked Jack.

"Nothin' to teach. You get out in the water, climb on the board, wait for a wave n' stand up," said Kai.

"Oh you're no help. Put our boards on the sand between the Jeeps and you guys go ahead n' paddle out," said Val. She turned toward Rachel. "It's easier to learn the basics onshore before you go out there. Kai's always in a rush."

"Have you been doing this a long time?" asked Rachel.

"Same as Kai. We both started when we were five. I think Jack was about seven, but he's pretty good. Don't worry; you'll get the hang of it."

Jack and Kai paddled beyond the breakers while Val stayed on the beach demonstrating the basics and coaching Rachel through the moves. Fifteen minutes later, they joined the boys.

"Okay first practice getting in front of the waves and ride a few into shore without trying to stand up. You gotta get the timing down. I'll ride in the same way and tell you when to dig. That means paddle as hard as you can," said Val.

"Do ya think she'll stand up by the end of the summer?" asked Kai.

"I'll bet she rides one all the way in by the end of the day," answered Jack.

"Yeah right. Talia never got it."

"Hah! The porcelain princess worried too much about her hair to get the footwork down."

"Uh oh. Tryin' to tell me somethin'?"

"Nope."

Rachel tensed. Everyone watched as she paddled with all her might to get in front of a good-sized roller. The wave started to curl as she planted her hands to the outside edge of the surfboard and pulled up to a kneeling position. Three, two one… she stood, putting her left foot ahead of her right, feet spread slightly, knees bent, arms away from her sides, turning the board with her front foot as she picked up speed. She stayed in front, fighting to keep her balance. It was a long ride, an unexpected and exhilarating success on her very first try.

Val yelled out encouragement and let loose with ear shattering whistles using two fingers between her lips. Kai and Jack stared open-mouthed as Rachel stayed upright through the foam.

Kai looked at Jack, then at Rachel as she tucked the board under her arm to wade back into the surf. "She's a keeper."

Jack kept his eyes trained straight ahead. "How'd Val ever learn to whistle like that? Not very ladylike."

"Gonna ignore me, right?"

"Yep."

They surfed for two hours before taking a break. Rachel had taken her share of spills after the first ride but continued to gain confidence on the board and with her new friends.

Kai sat cross-legged on the sand and leaned back on his elbows. He was muscular, not as tall and broad-shouldered as Jack, but well defined. His tan made everyone, Val included, look pale, and, in Rachel's case, almost sickly. Val was with Jack rummaging through a cooler in the back of Jack's Jeep. Rachel flipped her surfboard over and sat down across from Kai. Her arms and legs were tight and she could feel the sting of sunburn. When Kai straightened his right leg, Rachel noticed a long jagged scar just above the knee.

"What happened to your leg?"

Kai covered it with his hand. "It's nothin'. Happened awhile back."

Jack started to say something when Val interrupted. "Are you sure this is the first time you ever surfed?" she said as she handed Rachel a bottle of water.

"Thanks, I could drink a gallon of this stuff right now. Yeah, first time. I used to snowboard, maybe that helped."

Half an hour later they were back in the water taking advantage of the last few decent waves. When they found themselves floating more than surfing, they paddled to shore and called it a day.

Val pulled on her cover-up. "Kai, do you mind riding with Jack? I'll drive Rachel in your Jeep."

"I don't care. Keys are on the floor," he answered.

Here we go, thought Rachel. This is where I get the third degree from Val so she can report to Jack's girlfriend.

The guys drove north toward the ramp that Rachel and Jack had used earlier. Val turned south.

"Why are we going this way?" asked Rachel.

"It's longer, about three miles to the next ramp. I love driving on the beach," said Val.

"And you want to talk to me alone."

"Well, I did want to clear something up."

"Thought so." Rachel felt defensive.

Val didn't notice. "Kai didn't want to tell you about his scar."

"I thought he looked uncomfortable about it, so I didn't want to pry."

"He didn't want to scare you."

"Scare me?"

"Maybe scare isn't the right word, but he didn't want to ruin your day. You were doin' great. None of us have ever seen anyone ride their first wave. It was amazing."

"So what's the big deal?"

"The scar is from a shark attack."

"And I guess he was surfing when it happened."

"Yes."

"So he thought if I knew, I'd get scared and stay out of the water."

"Something like that."

"Wow. And he's not afraid of sharks now?"

"Says he's not. They were up at a place called Talbot Island when it happened. He cut his arm. There was blood in the water and it attracted the shark. It was just a freak thing. Kai says the odds of running into another one are way unlikely now. You know, the lightning striking twice kind of thing?"

"You said they. I assume that means Jack was with him when it happened?"

"Jack's the one that saved his life."

"No wonder they're such good friends."

"More like brothers." Val turned toward Rachel as they reached the ramp to the roadway. "So whaddya feel like doin' tonight?"

"I don't know. Didn't think about it."

"How 'bout hangin' out with me and Nina? You'll like her."

"That sounds cool. What time?"

"I'll pick you up around seven."

"Is Kai going to let you use his Jeep?"

"He would but I'll take my mom's car." Val pulled up to the Rackham gates and punched in the code.

"Does everybody know the security code for this place?"

Val drove into the driveway. "Just the Rackham's, me and Kai."

"You must be special," teased Rachel.

"They've always treated me n' Kai like family."

Kai was waiting by the garage door. "Where've ya been?"

"We took the long way."

"No kiddin'."

Rachel climbed out of the Jeep. "See you at seven?"

"I'll blow the horn." Val stayed in the driver's seat.

"You're drivin'?" asked Kai as he jumped in the passenger side.

"Yep."

"Guess I'd better buckle-up then."

"Yep."

~5~
BAD LATITUDE

KAI TOSSED A PACK OF AA batteries into a nylon bag when he heard the screen door open. The stretching sound of the spring disappeared with the sound of heavy knocking. Jack sat at the table fumbling with tie wraps and a small flashlight.

"Wanna guess who this is?" asked Kai as he crossed the room to the door. He found Val and Rachel standing on the landing at the top of the stairs.

"Hey," said Val.

"Hey yourself. What're you doin' here?"

"I don't know. I tried to call but no one answered."

Kai reached down and patted his hands against the pockets of his cargo shorts. He looked at Val. "My phone must be in the Jeep. I'll go get it, and then you can call me back."

Val ignored him with a dismissive wave and walked into the apartment. Rachel followed. Jack never looked up as he clipped a tie wrap with a pair of snips. "I was wondering when you would make an appearance. You're like a bloodhound, always know when me n' Kai are up to no good," he said absently.

"I thought you said we could take Rachel for a tour of The Old Jail. Did something new and exciting come up?" asked Val.

"It's no big deal, Jack. If you have other plans, I don't mind," said Rachel.

Jack looked up. "I didn't know you were here, Rachel. Sorry."

"But it's okay to be rude to me?" asked Val, pretending her feelings were hurt.

Kai jumped in. "Rachel gets a free pass for one more week, after that, no mercy."

Val laughed at that and gave Kai a big hug.

"We're still going to The Old Jail. Getting the gear together now. It'll be cool," said Jack as he stuffed the flashlight into a backpack.

Val was suspicious. "The jail closes at six and what gear are you talking about?"

Jack shrugged and looked at Kai. "You care to explain?"

"Nope. I got up n' answered the door. Your turn."

"Okay. We're going just before midnight," announced Jack. "There will be more paranormal activity around the witching hour. The gear we're packing is for ghost hunting. How's that? Cover all your questions?"

Val played along. "So this is gonna be like last year at the lighthouse?"

"Sort of, but we have equipment this time so we can get proof that the place is haunted."

"You guys are kidding…right?" asked Rachel.

Kai tied the loops of the bag together as he answered. "Nobody's kiddin'. It's time for some adventure. You gonna bail on us?"

"I told you these guys are nuts. We don't have to go," said Val.

"What did you mean about the lighthouse?" asked Rachel.

"Oh that. We bumped into a couple of dead girls and their bearded daddy one night when we climbed the lighthouse stairs. He was a ghost too," answered Val.

Rachel suspected a prank and smiled. "Count me in. It's been ages since I've run across a real ghost."

"Cool. You guys can help us get the rest of this stuff ready. We want to divide everything into two backpacks so we get the best coverage and split into pairs. Better to have everything all tested and wired up in advance," said Jack as he tore open the wrapper on a small rectangular box. The label said it contained one EMF Meter. On the table sat a not yet opened camcorder claiming night-vision capabilities.

"You're serious," said Rachel unable to disguise the dread in her voice.

Val laughed. "You thought this was a joke? Rachel, this is nothin'. By the end of this summer, you won't be scared of anything ever again."

"Yeah, tough guy over there will hold your hand," added Kai.

Jack ignored him. "We studied up on paranormal investigation stuff. I've got friends in Indianapolis that are into it and they hooked me up with this cool gear. They have a company called Paranormal 911. Last year, when we ran into those ghosts, all I had was a cheap digital camera. Most of the pictures were blurred, but I did get one shot where the faces showed up. That was before they grabbed me. I don't remember much after that," explained Jack.

Rachel sat on the chair opposite Jack. "Grabbed you? They actually grabbed you?"

"Well, yeah. Kai and Val can tell you all about it. No big deal. Since ghosts don't have bodies, they can't really hurt you. I don't think they can anyway. All we want to do is prove the place is haunted and make contact. Nothing to worry about," said Jack.

"He wouldn't say that if he saw what those sister spooks were doin' last year," said Kai.

"Would you knock it off Kai? You're gonna scare her," Val scolded.

Rachel didn't want any part of ghost hunting but wasn't about to wimp out. As an outsider with no friends or family, she was grateful they had accepted her into their circle. "I'll be okay. It sounds like fun. Are we really allowed in there at night?" she asked.

"Yep. The tour manager gave me the keys. I offered to do two things. Give them a complete copy of everything we film and record and donate a fee toward some maintenance projects that they're planning. It's totally cool," said Jack.

"You mean you bribed him?" asked Rachel.

"Yes. I made the offer and he cleared it with the management company in Key West. It's all in writing. Everybody wins and no one gets in trouble. Unless something grabs us, then we'll be in trouble," answered Jack.

"So was The Old Jail really a…"

Kai interrupted. "Me n' Val need to hit the road. I can tell when you're gettin' ready to tell a story and I'm not hangin' out for that. This bag's all ready to go. We'll meet you guys in the parkin' lot at eleven-thirty." With a quick goodbye, Val and Kai walked out leaving Jack and Rachel alone for the first time since Jack had found her rummaging through the garbage can.

After a few awkward minutes, Jack picked up the conversation. "You asked if The Old Jail was really a prison. It used to be the St. Johns County Jail, built in 1891, with donations from the millionaire Henry Flagler, to replace the one downtown next to his Hotel Ponce de Leon. He didn't think his rich friends and guests would like staying next door to a bunch of murderers and horse thieves. It held a maximum number of seventy two inmates plus the Warden and his family."

"A family lived there? Do you really know this stuff or are you making it up?"

"It's all true. The family had nice living quarters separated from the bad guys by a pair of wooden doors but, yes, they were in the same building. When things were busy, the tiny cells were crowded with four prisoners, one to a bunk. There were no mattresses, no screens or glass over the barred windows, and, for a long time, no indoor plumbing. Conditions were pretty disgusting."

"Did they have an electric chair?" asked Rachel.

"No, they used a wooden gallows in the back for hangings. There's one there now but it's a replica. I don't think they had too many executions, but they did have a maximum security section and solitary confinement area. Can you imagine how hot and smelly it would be in the summer and how cold and wet during heavy rainstorms?"

"And buggy," added Rachel.

"Really buggy," Jack agreed. "It closed up in 1953 and the county turned it into a tourist attraction. It's all real, except for the inmates; they're made out of fiberglass or something. There's also a mechanical version of Sheriff Joe Perry, the jail's most famous warden. He stands on a platform and sternly explains the prison rules to tourists while local actors, pretending to be deputies, lead everyone through the place like prisoners. According to history, Sheriff Perry was an enormous man, so they made the robot-like attraction life-sized. At the end, the guides abandon the visitors, leaving them to find their own escape route. It's pretty cool."

"So why the interest in something like The Old Jail, especially after spending most of the night in one a few days ago?"

"They didn't keep me in a cell with bars."

"Answer the question. Why?"

Jack thought about it for a moment. "I don't know. It's another adventure, like last year's visit to the lighthouse."

Rachel sighed. "So you guys were serious about the dead girls. You weren't making it up. And now you're really going ghost hunting."

"Those spirits were real and that story is totally true. Here's the deal. I like to take risks. Watching movies, playing video games and hanging out is fine once in awhile but too much of it bores me to death. Kai's the same way. We surf and kite board & run around in the boat, all that normal stuff, but it's not enough. Maybe we won't live to be old men, but we're gonna have a blast for as long as we can, doing stuff most people would never try."

"You're crazy you know."

"Yeah, maybe, but it's paid off so far," said Jack with a smirk.

"What's that supposed to mean?"

"It's a long story."

"So tell me."

"Are you up for a trip on Bad Latitude?"

"What?"

"Bad Latitude. That's my boat. We'll take a spin and I'll tell you the story."

"You mean just the two of us?" asked Rachel.

"What's the matter, you think I'm some kind of psycho?"

"You're probably a little psycho, but that's not the point. I'm not afraid of you, but aren't you worried that Val will blab about our boat ride to your girlfriend? It sounds like the two of them are pretty tight."

Jack ignored the question. "We're wasting daylight. If you want to take a river run and hear the story, we'd better get going," said Jack.

They walked from the apartment to the dock and Jack punched in the code to lower the hydraulic lift that held his boat. In a few minutes, they were underway, moving south, slowly at first. Jack stood at the helm while Rachel sat in the swivel seat to his left.

"Are you holding on?"

"Yeah. Why?"

"Just checkin'," said Jack as he throttled to full speed. He was surprised when Rachel abandoned her seat to stand next to him and he turned to watch her reaction. She was smiling; head tilted with chin held high, celebrating the wind in her face as it flowed through her long blonde hair. It was the look of relief. It was the look of worried happiness. Jack felt a brief stab of pity for her, and fought the urge to put a reassuring arm around her shoulder. He didn't want to send the wrong message and faced forward, abruptly stuffing his hand in the pocket of his cargo shorts.

It was a ten-minute ride to Rattlesnake Island. The tide was running out and Jack held Bad Latitude in place twenty feet from shore just out of the channel and set the anchor off the bow. The depth finder showed six feet of water below the hull. He flipped the switches on for the running lights and shut down the engine before producing two cold bottles of Vitamin Water and a pair of binoculars. After handing one bottle to Rachel and giving her the follow me sign, he climbed over the front seat to slide onto the point of the bow dangling his legs over the side below the stainless rails. She hopped across and sat beside him thinking it was an odd place to drop anchor.

"This is Rattlesnake Island," said Jack as he handed Rachel the binoculars.

She stared through the lenses trying to see if there was something she was missing. Finally, she said, "I don't see anything but tall grass and small shrubs. What am I looking for?"

"Nothing. Fort Matanzas is on the eastern side but you won't see it past the palmettos."

"So what's the point?" asked Rachel.

"This is where me n' Kai spent lots of time last summer, out there in that grass, surrounded by poisonous snakes, trying to find a fortune in gold and gemstones hidden away in the forgotten Indian burial grounds." Jack proceeded to share with Rachel the story about their search, the chase and the treasure. After more than an hour, with dusk settling in, it was time to head back.

"So you and Kai were almost killed, but you're millionaires," said Rachel as she watched Jack hoist the anchor.

"Yeah, but we don't tell anyone, so don't repeat any of this," said Jack.

"I'd never say a word. Besides, who'd be dumb enough to believe me?"

"Good point. Time to go, it's getting late."

～6～
THE OLD JAIL

∽THEY WERE WAITING IN THE parking lot when Jack and Rachel arrived. Val looked toward Kai with one raised eyebrow. "Wonder what's up with those two. He's usually early for everything."

"Awww don't even go there," replied Kai.

"It's not lookin' good for Talia these days is it?" she persisted

Kai ignored the comment and jumped out of his Jeep as Jack pulled into the neighboring parking space. "Where've you guys been? It's almost midnight."

"I forgot the equipment bag that you packed. We made it halfway up Anastasia Island when I realized it and had to run back to the house," said Jack.

"Sounds like a pretty fishy excuse to me," said Val. She caught the mortified look on Rachel's face and regretted the comment immediately. "Sorry. Not funny."

"You're right, it wasn't funny," said Jack icily. He fished a set of keys and a mini flashlight from his pocket and jogged to the back door of the jail leaving the others to grab the bags.

Kai started to say something but Rachel cut him off and turned toward Val. "When you make your report to Talia, make sure she knows there's nothing to worry about. I'm not interested and I don't plan on hanging around very long." She grabbed one of the backpacks and ran to catch up with Jack.

The Old Jail and Gallows—Saint Augustine, Florida

"Nice one," said Kai as he lifted the remaining bag from Jack's Jeep.

Val felt the tears welling up. She hadn't intended to hurt Rachel's feelings. "I'll talk to her later. I meant it as a joke, but I should have known better. She thinks I'm a spy for Talia and Jack thinks I'm a jerk."

Kai wanted to stay out of it. "Let's get goin'. We can talk about it later."

Val and Kai caught up as Jack pulled the rear door open. He grabbed the bag from Rachel, walked a few feet into the jail and knelt down. With the small flashlight clenched between his teeth, he rummaged through the duffel. "Here Rachel, you can handle the DAR. Flip this switch forward when I give you the word and hold it away from your body about twelve to eighteen inches. When you aim it toward ... whatever we find... try to move it slowly."

"What's a DAR?" whispered Rachel.

"It's a Digital Audio Recorder. This type lets you separate sounds on the recording. The camera will pick up sound too, but not as detailed and it's harder to retrieve," said Jack. "What do you want Kai, the video camera or the EMF meter?"

"I'll take the video. The night vision setting's gonna be cool. By the way, why are we all whisperin'?"

Jack handed Kai the recorder and grinned. "Because whispering makes it scarier. Okay Val. That leaves you the EMF meter or the Infrared Thermometer, your choice."

"Gimme the EMF."

"What does the EMF thing do?" asked Rachel, still whispering, making Kai chuckle.

"The EMF measures the electromagnetic field. Ghosts put off a type of radiation and this gizmo measures and tracks movement. Some ghosts move around or shift things in a room to communicate. Others make sounds. Between the DAR and EMF equipment, we should have all the bases covered. That's about it. I'll carry the bag with batteries and other stuff and take the point with the thermometer and the small flashlight. You guys keep a flashlight in your pockets for emergencies but don't turn them on unless you have to. Kai, you bring up the rear and keep Val and Rachel between us. Stay spaced about six feet apart so the equipment will work the way it's supposed to. Everybody set?"

Rachel was nervous but it didn't keep her from smiling. A few days earlier she had been all alone and now she was in the middle of a ghost hunt, like it was a routine adventure.

They walked through the corridor between the first floor cells. The darkness closed in as they traveled deeper. Jack had the mini flashlight partially covered with his hand, minimizing the effect, aiming it toward the floor while Kai used the night vision accessory of the video camera to scan the cells and check the corridor behind. No one spoke until they reached the cross corridor. Thunder rumbled in the distance.

"Here we go. Hear that? What'd you do Rackham, pay extra for the thunder?" asked Kai.

"I checked the weather. It was supposed to be clear all night."

Val looked over at Rachel. "Gotta be a hoax. They probably planted sound effects to scare us."

Rachel's heart was pounding but she was determined to act confident. "Cool. Maybe we'll get some lightning to go with it."

Kai spoke up. "Here's the light switches, I'm gonna turn on my mini light & hang it here. If anyone gets too creeped out or somethin' happens, run over here and flip the lights on. Nobody's gonna get mad if that happens. Sometimes this ghost stuff gets pretty intense."

Val laughed. "More hocus pocus. So are we telling scary stories or are we gonna start hunting?"

"Now we split into pairs. Start upstairs and we'll work our way down. If we pick up anything odd on the EMF or the thermometer, we'll get back together. Val and Rachel can take the north end and we'll take the south. Only one person at a time can try to summon a spirit, so you guys pick between the two of you which one will do the talking," said Jack.

"No way! You and Kai are going to leave us on our own?" protested Val.

"I gave everyone their choice of equipment. You have the EMF and I have the thermometer. Kai and Rachel have the recording devices. There's nothing to record if we don't track the energy."

"Why didn't you explain that at the start?"

"It's okay, Val. Let's just get going. I can do the talking if you want," said Rachel as she started up the concrete steps.

At the top of the stairs, positioned on a balcony was the mechanical version of Sheriff Joe Perry. The girls had to pass behind the massive fiberglass statue while Jack and Kai went in the opposite direction. Visibility was slightly better as more light filtered through the second floor windows. The thunder clapped, accompanied by blinding flashes of lightning. Shadows danced across the walls.

From the cell in the south corner, Jack tried to communicate as he held the probe out toward the walls. "Is anyone here? Hello? If anyone is here, speak to us. Let us know you're here." He repeated this several times, as he inched his way through the cells.

On the south end, Val and Rachel started in the furthermost cell. They could hear Jack's voice echoing through the corridor. Rachel decided to take a more confrontational approach. "I know someone is in here. Show yourself if you have the guts," she hissed.

"What are you t-t-trying to do? Are you outta your mind?" asked Val.

"Might as well stir 'em up good," replied Rachel.

The storm moved in from the northeast and wind gusted through the bars at the windows. The lightning and thunder intensified. Driving rain would soon follow. Rachel felt exhilarated. She had to prove to herself that she was unafraid and moved boldly into the next cell. "What are you scared of?" she yelled mockingly into the darkness.

Val's hands shook as she aimed the EMF around the tiny cell. It wasn't the lightning or the chance of a paranormal encounter that had her worried, it was Rachel. The look on the girl's face and the way she challenged the spirits terrified her.

She started again, pleading with Rachel to back off when the EMF lights began to glow. The machine hummed, softly at first, before building to a painfully high-pitched squeal. As Val reached for the switch, she felt the heat on her fingers and threw the EMF Meter onto a steel bunk. Her fingers were slightly blistered and she wanted to scream but couldn't make a sound. Something covered her mouth from behind, pulling her roughly toward the bars of the iron door. She watched in horror as a shape appeared at the end of the cell. Rachel stared straight ahead, unaware that Val was in trouble. Her hair blew back from her face and her soft green eyes changed to a gleaming yellow as she reached her hand toward the glowing shadow.

"Sounds like those two are really into it," laughed Kai as they moved to another cell.

"Is that Rachel or Val yelling down there?" asked Jack.

"I can't tell. Maybe you should get loud like them," said Kai.

"Maybe we should go check on them."

"I'll run down there. You take the video camera. Can't use the night vision with all this lightning," answered Kai.

"Alright, I'll keep moving along down here."

Kai made it partway down the corridor. Sheriff Perry had moved from the balcony to block the walkway to the north end. The face had changed. It looked angry. "Nobody escapes my jailhouse," it said as one of its massive arms began to move.

"Hey, Rackham, how'd you manage this trick?" yelled Kai over the thunder.

"What are you yappin' about?"

"Movin' the Sheriff, you dimwit. How'd you pull this off?"

Jack abandoned the cell to see what Kai was talking about. "No wonder we can't find anything… What the…"

"Stop actin' like you had nothin' to do with this. How do you shut it off?" ask Kai as he approached the moving statue.

"Kai, I didn't do anything. Stay away from it!"

"It's me remember? I could see you pullin' a stunt like this on the girls, but I ain't fallin' for it." Kai shook his head and laughed as he moved toward Sheriff Perry. "How much didja spend to rig this up anyway? It's one of your better efforts, I'll give ya that," he shouted.

The robotic arm of the Sheriff reached out in a grabbing motion causing Kai to hesitate. A moment later he found himself on the floor being tugged backwards by the collar. Jack helped him off the floor but maintained the tight hold on the shirt. "I didn't rig anything."

"Yeah right. You don't hafta choke me to death to prove it."

"Quiet! I don't hear anything from the other end. Do you think Val and Rachel are in trouble?" asked Jack.

"You tryin' to change the subject? I'm not fallin' for it so lemme go," barked Kai.

"I'm going for the lights downstairs. This is out of control. Don't go near that thing."

"You think actin' all serious is gonna scare me," laughed Kai. "Just 'cause you got me with the snake trick last year. I'm not believin' ya this time."

"Stay away from it. I can't get past it to reach the stairs so I'll climb over the rail and drop down. Hold my flashlight so I can see what I'm doing and keep an eye on that thing." Jack handed over the light and stretched his legs over the rail, lowering himself so that his hands held onto the bottom of a steel post leaving an eight-foot drop to the floor below. As he let go, he heard a scream.

Val struggled against the unseen grip, finally twisting loose and collapsing to the floor. She screamed at Rachel to back away, but it was too late. A blinding light filled the room as Rachel made contact with the spirit.

Jack flipped on all of the light switches but everything remained dark. The power was out. He charged up the stairs yelling to Kai that the girls were in trouble. As he reached the top step, he dove beneath the outstretched arm of the mechanical Sheriff Perry, rolled across the concrete floor and jumped to his feet. He sprinted down the corridor toward the white light at the end of the cellblock. As he raced through the doorway of the cell, he tripped over Val, crashing headfirst into the steel frame of an upper bunk before falling backwards with a thud onto the floor. Ignoring the pain and the warm flow of blood running into his right eye from a gash to his forehead, he pulled himself up and reached for Rachel. As he stood and leaned forward, something smashed into him from behind and he slammed face first into the same steel bunk. Jack crawled forward on his knees, wrapped his left arm around Rachel's waist and pulled her backwards, away from the end of the cell. The connection with the spirit was broken and the brilliant light blinked out.

Jack shook Rachel gently. "Are you okay?" She was dazed, shivering slightly and didn't reply, her arms were coated with a dusting of light frost.

Kai helped Val to her feet and moved next to Jack before aiming the flashlight between Jack and Rachel. He was the first to notice the blood flowing freely from Jack's face. "We need to get outta here, Jack. You're gonna need stitches and Rachel looks like she's in shock."

"I'm okay. She's coming around," answered Jack. "Rachel, are you alright?"

"I think so," she said, still shaking. "That was so weird. It was trying to communicate with me. I wasn't really scared. It was kind of peaceful, but, whatever it was, it needs our help."

"Great. We've got a real live ghost whisperer with us," cracked Kai as he tightened his arm across Val's shoulders. "We need to leave. The ghost thing is gonna hafta get help from somebody else. Jack's bleedin' all over the place and I don't know how we're gettin' past that dummy blockin' the stairs."

Val spoke for the first time. "We've got all the gear with us. Let's see if we can get a recording and find out what it wants. We might never get a chance like this again."

"She's right," said Jack as he mopped the blood from his face. "Kai, turn on the DAR and see what we get. Rachel, the spirit was trying to talk to you, so you ask the questions. We'll download everything back at the house and see what this spirit-thing wants."

"You guys are nuts," said Kai as he aimed the recorder toward the back wall. "What about old Sheriff Perry down the hall?"

"We'll deal with him later. Shine the light toward the steps and see if he's moving this way. Val, are you getting any readings on the EMF?"

"The EMF is lit up in solid red. That means we still have company and the ghost is right there next to the window," said Val.

"Great. Everything clear in the corridor?"

"Yep. The big guy is back where he's supposed to be," said Kai. "Let's get this done."

"Rachel, are you okay with this?" asked Jack.

"Yeah. What do you want me to ask?"

Jack coached Rachel through the questions while Kai handled the recorder. Val aimed the EMF in all directions, but the signal remained strongest at the window. The recorder showed sound waves as they were received, though no one would hear the answers to the questions until filtering was finished. Rachel relayed Jack's questions for more than twenty-five minutes. Finally, the EMF blinked back to green and the recorder stopped registering responses. The phantom was gone.

"Well, looks like that's our show for tonight boys n' girls," said Kai. "Now we just need an escape plan."

The words were barely out of his mouth when the lights flickered on.

"Guess that means it's time to go," said Val.

Rachel looked at Jack, seeing, for the first time, the damage above his eyebrow. "Look at your face! We need to get you to an emergency room."

"I'm okay!"

"You need stitches! How did that happen?" asked Rachel.

"I tripped over something running into the cell and smashed into one of the steel bunks."

"That would have been me," said Val.

"What would have been you?" asked Jack.

"I was on the floor and you tripped over me."

"Well, whatever was here didn't want me in the cell with you guys. As soon as I got up, it smashed me from behind into the same bunk."

"That would've been me," said Kai.

Jack sighed. "What would have been you?"

"I tripped over Val when I ran in, hit you in the back and knocked you into the bunk the second time. Kinda funny, huh?"

"So the ghost was the good guy all along and my best friends were the ones trying to kill me," said Jack as he looked from Kai to Val.

"The ghost was a woman," whispered Rachel.

Kai eyed her suspiciously. "How do you know that?"

"I'm not sure, but I know her name … is Mary."

"Let's get outta here. We'll see if Mary had anything to say on the recorder," said Jack.

Rachel gasped as she pointed toward Jack. "The cut on your forehead is …"

"I'm okay," said Jack. He raised his hand to his head. "It feels like there's ice on it."

"But it's healing all by itself," said Val. "It's…it's disappearing."

The mechanized version of Joe Perry stayed where it belonged but the four squeezed past hugging the far wall, just in case. Jack hit the lights while the others waited at the back door. Twenty minutes later, they climbed the stairs to the boathouse apartment. Kai and Val hooked up the digital recorder to the laptop. It was nearly three in the morning when the filtering was completed. They listened as the spirit answered Rachel's questions. Two hours later, they were still trying to make sense of it.

"Okay, we know she was in jail for stealing a…chicken?"

"Why is that important?" asked Val.

"She's trying to convince us that she wasn't a bad person," said Rachel.

"I don't think that's as important as the part where she says *Joe Perry died*," said Jack. "That's the key."

Val tried to stifle a yawn. "Maybe we should have a séance."

"No way. I ain't gettin' into that weird crap," said Kai. "Rackham, you n' Pop are always talkin' about usin' history to chase down clues. There must be some kind of records to check."

"Joe Perry died. Joe Perry d... Wait a minute. He's right!" said Rachel.

Kai looked surprised. "I am? Geez, twice in one night."

Rachel stood and walked partway across the room before turning to face the others. "Find out when Joe Perry died and see if there's a list of prisoners from that date. I'll bet we find an inmate named Mary that's logged in as a chicken thief."

"Let's assume you're right. What can we do about it? She says she's trapped with the others and Joe Perry died. How do we help a ghost, or worse, a whole bunch of ghosts, escape?" asked Jack.

Val looked up. "Listen to the tape one more time."

"We've gone over it a gazillion times already, Val. I gotta take a break," complained Kai.

"Just once. You know where the important part is. Jump ahead to that."

Kai hit the back button on the lap top and scrolled with the mouse. "Here ya go. Last time, then I'm outta here."

The voice was a high-pitched wail, the words delivered in choppy bunches. The filters removed only part of the distortion, making it difficult for all four to reach agreement on the interpretation. Words such as Mary, thief, us, trapped, Perry, and died were the clearest.

"Maybe we need better equipment," said Val.

"What if she's not saying Joe Perry died? What if she's saying 'When Perry died'?" asked Rachel.

"I think we should all take a break. Right now I'm so tired I'm hearing more than voices," said Kai. "Val, let's get goin'."

"Kai's right. We're all beat. Even if we solve what's on the tape, we still don't know what we can do to help the old chicken thief," said Jack. "I'll see if Pop can help me get more information on Sheriff Perry and whatever jailhouse records might be around. He's good at that stuff."

"Yeah, real good," agreed Kai.

"If we could just travel back in time, we could break her out of jail," said Rachel.

"There's a thought," laughed Kai.

Val and Kai drove off as Rachel walked through the back door into the main house. Jack sat down at the computer trying to pull up historical records. Two hours later, he was printing out pages from the county archives, reports and stories from the early days of 1919.

C J "Joe" Perry was born in 1863 and died February 7th, 1919. He served as sheriff twice, from 1889 until 1897 and again beginning in 1901 until his death in 1919. According to all accounts, he was an honest and dedicated public servant, determined to maintain order and uphold county law. At six feet six inches and three hundred twenty pounds, he was an imposing figure, regarded by the public as fair-minded and good-hearted. On the day of Joe Perry's death, only fourteen prisoners occupied St. John's County jail, a small number for those days. Two of the inmates were women, one being the accused chicken thief, Mary Barrett.

Mary's arrest was the result of a longstanding feud between neighbors. When Elsa Walker hacked off the head of one of her chickens, to prepare it for the evening meal, the headless bird ran south into the yard of Mary Barrett, finally collapsing at the bottom step of the Barrett porch. Mary, in plain sight of her neighbor, retrieved the feathered corpse, plucked it clean and waved the dead bird at the always-spiteful Elsa before taking it inside the house to cook the chicken for herself. Mrs. Walker was the wife of a local merchant, a mean-spirited man of influence in St Augustine who owned the drug store on Cordova Street. At Elsa's insistence, her husband pressed charges. Sheriff Perry, according to his own journal, reluctantly arrested Mary and placed her in a ground floor cell on January 10th to serve a thirty-day sentence.

Without heat, and with only bars filling the window openings, the raw damp weather took its toll and Mrs. Barrett developed pneumonia. Documents showed that Sheriff Perry pleaded for her early release, arguing that life-saving medical attention couldn't be put off. Mr. Walker and his circle of cronies stubbornly rejected his requests, demanding that Mary serve the full thirty-day sentence.

The records were clear that on the night of February 7th, Joe Perry died. Hours later, just past midnight on the eighth, two days before her scheduled release date, Mary Barrett also passed away, with no recorded documentation of the cause of death.

What Jack did not discover from the records was the fact that, as Mary took her last rasping breath, hot embers from the cast iron stove in the Walker kitchen swirled around in a steady noiseless breeze and scattered across the wooden floor. No one inside escaped as the embers ignited and the house burned to the ground. At daybreak, neighbors gathered around the pile of smoldering rubble and stared silently as a bleeding headless chicken strutted atop the glowing ashes. They never recovered the bodies of the Walkers, but a legend was born.

To this day, chickens roam wild through parts of St. Augustine, protected from harm or capture by local ordinance. Life-long residents commonly refer to these chickens as *Walkers*.

~7~
RECKLESS ENDEAVOR

POP WAS LESS SKILLED AT WAITING than fishing. Frustrated, he held his thumb against the horn button for long bursts of ear splitting blasts. Jack arrived on the run three minutes later carrying his shoes and shirt. A blue toothbrush poked out from the side of his mouth.

"Sorry. I overslept."

"I'm surprised you slept at all. Your friends left at daybreak. What were you guys up to that late?" asked Pop.

Jack told Pop the story about their trip to the Old Jail and how they pieced together clues about one of the inmates now haunting the place.

"What is it with you n' dead folks? Ya can't make any money chasin' ghosts."

Jack chuckled as Pop fired up the engine. "Did okay last year."

"Yeah, that was probably a fluke. Where is everybody? I said ten o'clock. Can't y'all tell time anymore?"

"It's only 9:55."

Val and Kai had no clue about what to expect as they drove through the gates of the estate. Nan had asked them to stop by no later than ten. Kai wanted to know if the invitation had something to do with the upcoming trip. Nan replied *yes* and hung up abruptly.

They found Jack, Rachel and Nan standing on the dock next to the deck boat, which idled in the water with Pop waiting at the controls.

"Come on. Come on. Don't waste time standin' there; we're goin' for a short boat ride."

Everyone climbed aboard and Pop backed away from the dock before turning upriver toward St. Augustine. Within twenty minutes, they were cruising beneath the newly refurbished Bridge of Lions. Pop made a subtle call on his cell phone before advancing toward the inlet. He edged the deck boat toward the eastern shoreline and shoved the throttle back to neutral, with the bow pointed toward the opening of the Matanzas Bay. They paused only briefly, long enough to watch as a schooner with a pair of tall masts, fully rigged with billowing sails, passed through the inlet into the bay. *Reckless Endeavor* had arrived. As the massive vessel came into view, Pop, with his arm draped across Nan's shoulder, winked at Jack. "Whaddya think?"

Reckless Endeavor sat high in the water and knifed through the light swells effortlessly. The sound of the seawater slapping against the wooden hull mixed with the noisy snap of her wind-filled sails carried across the water, drowning out the sound of nearby boat motors. She was a square-rigged two-masted schooner, unusual for modern day sailors who preferred the single curved variety. Two sets hung from each mast, the smaller above the larger with four headsails tied smartly to the bowsprit. Atop the mainmast, the Rackham flag flew proudly, a white skull poised above crossed cutlasses, centered against a background of jet-black, which stood out regally against the cloudless powder-blue sky. It was a replica of the flag flown by Jack's infamous eighteenth-century ancestor, Calico Jack Rackham. Across the stern, written in sweeping gold-leaf calligraphy the name, *Reckless Endeavor.*

Jack turned his head from his grandparents to the sailboat several times as if to verify that what he was staring at was real. Kai, Val and Rachel knelt on the bow cushions, eyes fixed on the majestic vessel as it crossed into the Matanzas. Traffic in the waterway came to a standstill as boaters stopped to make way and watch the grand schooner glide gracefully toward the historic bayside fortress that guarded the Ancient City.

Pop throttled forward and pulled alongside to observe the smooth furling of the sails. Once tucked away, Pop waved to the captain and pointed out the mooring buoy positioned a hundred yards east of the seawall at the Castillo de San Marcos. He circled behind the schooner's stern as the big boat aimed its bow to face the current and motioned for Jack to take the wheel before moving to the bow. "Get us lined up with her nose to nose. Stay back about ten or twelve feet, I'm going to grab the pennant and hook her to the buoy," ordered Pop.

With *Reckless Endeavor* safely secured, Pop swung the deck boat around to the port side, positioned the plastic fenders to protect the hulls from banging together, and tossed a pair of lines to the crew above to tie off the smaller craft. A rope ladder rolled down from over the side of the sailboat's deck. Nan was the first to climb aboard, followed by Pop. They wanted to be topside to see everyone's expression as they boarded.

"I'm seeing, but not believing," said Jack as he absorbed the view from bow to stern. "Pop, I knew it would be spectacular but never pictured anything like this. It's amazing."

The schooner had been restored to her former magnificence, with several disguised improvements. All of the decking had been replaced with solid teak, as were the gunwales and trimmings. The reinforced hull was overlaid with thick oak planking with wooden pegs placed to hide the stainless bolts that secured the planks to the unseen frame. Pop had ordered all of the rigging and ratlines changed to heavy black nylon, rather than the hemp favored in earlier times. Brass cleats and hardware had been removed, painstakingly swapped for stainless steel for the sake of durability, the rare concession to practicality in exchange for authenticity. In the center of the cockpit was the helm, with its original wooden wheel, detailed to pristine condition but surrounded by the latest in navigational equipment and technology. A protective fiberglass shell, clad in teak surrounded the modern gadgetry camouflaging the screens and instruments from the casual observer.

"Kids, this is Captain Ron Sutton. He not only sailed her from Rhode Island, he's the man that put this baby together," announced Pop as he shook hands with the Captain. "You already know Deb. This is my grandson Jack and his friends Kai, Val and Rachel. How'd she handle for you, Ron? Do you think we need to make any changes?"

Captain Sutton smiled and clapped Pop on the shoulder. He was about the same height as Pop, just under six feet, and had deep lines etched in his tanned face from years of sailing through all types of weather. His reddish hair, mixed with white, was thick and tied in a ponytail. Like Pop, he had a goatee, though his was not neatly trimmed. "Mr. Rackham, this little dingy couldn't have sailed better. I wouldn't change a thing. We sailed through some rough seas off Cape May and Henlopen but she never flinched. This is a fine vessel and I'm sure she'll serve you well. To make up some time, we ran the…"

Pop interrupted. "Ron, hold that thought if you don't mind. I don't want to get too caught up in that stuff at the moment. That's more for me n' Jack anyway. Would you mind giving my grandson and his friends a tour of the deck?" In a whisper, Pop said to Captain Sutton, "I don't want to mention any of the *special features* just yet. I'm savin' that for later. Let's stick to the basics, if you don't mind."

Jack and his friends followed Captain Sutton as he showed them around topside while Pop and Nan walked on their own. "What's the big secret about the engines?" asked Nan.

Pop leaned against the starboard rail and gazed across the bay toward the ocean. "I thought about it this morning. Right now, everyone thinks she's just a pretty sailboat. If word gets out, you know, if one of the kids tells the wrong person, that *Reckless* is more than she appears, it could spell trouble before we even leave port."

"Oh I think you're being paranoid. No one's going to…well, now that I think of it, you might be right. This could be just the right toy for the wrong people. As I recall, Kai has a tough time keeping things quiet when he's excited," conceded Nan.

"Ron and his two guys will stay aboard until we're done with the sea trials and training. When that's done, it'll probably take a week; we'll move her to the marina and tie her up at the end of the dock. That'll make it easier to load our gear and provisions. I ain't climbin' that rope ladder any more than I have to," said Pop. At that moment, he spotted one of the crewmembers. The man was eavesdropping and Pop wondered how the man had managed to station himself within earshot totally undetected. This gave Pop an eerie feeling and, when he turned to make conversation, the deckhand walked off hurriedly toward the stern.

"Did you notice that guy standing off to my right?" asked Pop.

Nan looked puzzled. "What guy?"

"One of Sutton's men. I think he was trying to listen to our conversation."

"Now I really think you're paranoid."

"I saw him tryin' to hide so he could listen. The guy gave me the creeps."

"Oh come on. What could he want to hear?" asked Nan.

"Maybe he'd like to know our destination. There's somethin' not right about 'im."

"How could you tell all of that if you only saw him for a second?"

"I can read people. See things in their eyes. And that's one problem. His eyes had no color. They were lifeless. He's all muscled up, with tattoos of snakes wrapping down both arms and he was wearin' gloves," said Pop.

"You saw all of that in a split second? Maybe he just has light colored eyes. Sometimes, the pigment of the iris is very pale, particularly with people with very light hair. And having tattoos or wearing gloves doesn't make someone a bad guy. You have a couple of tattoos and sometimes you wear gloves. Last time I checked, you weren't such a bad guy." Nan turned to face the water.

"His hair is jet black with a thick streak of white on the left side. There's no explanation for the gloves. There's no work going on. Why wear 'em? The guy panicked when I made eye contact. He couldn't wait to make himself scarce. Most people caught evesdroppin', would say hello, or smile or nod, at least act embarrassed. They wouldn't just turn and hurry away unless they had somethin' to hide. I'm gonna ask Sutton about him later, find out what the guy is all about," said Pop. "Maybe it's nothin', but I'm not takin' any chances."

Nan tugged his arm and motioned toward the bow. "Let's catch up with the kids."

"So that's all there is too it," Captain Sutton was saying.

Kai stood with his arms folded across his chest."That's it huh? You make it sound like any idiot could sail this thing."

"Almost *any* idiot could sail her. Think you'd be up for the challenge?" asked the Captain.

"Depends on whether or not the teacher was a stone cold moron I guess. Think you'd be up to the job?" replied Kai.

Pop interrupted the conversation. "I see you two fellas are gettin' along about as well as I'd expected. Let's go below decks and check out the rest of this bucket before you guys start seein' who can climb the masts the fastest."

The words barely escaped Pop's mouth when Kai and Captain Sutton raced to the masts and started hoisting themselves up the ratlines toward the top. The Captain was in great shape, but no match for the much younger, more agile Kai. As Sutton breathlessly reached the top of the shorter mast, Kai, who had removed his shoes and shirt, offered another challenge. "Wanna race down to the deck headfirst?" The Captain declined with a hearty laugh and weary salute.

Jack yelled up from below. "Kai, all you proved was you're the second fastest climber on this boat. How 'bout a real race?"

Watching Captain Sutton on the downward climb, Kai reached for one of the lines left dangling from the masthead. "First let me get to the deck ahead of our teacher," he laughed.

Balancing himself on the yardarm, Kai prepared to rappel the forty-five feet to the deck below. As he leaned out to shake the line to make sure it was loose for its entire length, a breeze gusted and he toppled forward with the nylon line in hand. Rachel screamed as he flipped headfirst in her direction. Midway through the somersault, he gripped the rope with his left hand, stopping his descent and twisted into a swinging motion. Three seconds later he was standing next to Pop watching Sutton complete the climb from the mast.

"Must suck gettin' old huh, Cap'n Ron?" said Kai as Sutton's foot touched down.

Rachel surprised everyone and yelled at Kai. "You're crazy! You coulda killed yourself!"

Val interrupted. "Rachel, chill. This is just the beginning and if you're gonna get all hysterical on us every time these idiots act like…uhm…idiots, it'll be a long, miserable trip." She turned to Kai. "She's right. You are crazy and coulda killed yourself showing off like that!"

Captain Sutton shook his head. "I was young once. Nice job of reminding me kid."

Nan shook her head. "You're all nuts. Let's go below where it's safe, I hope."

Jack elbowed Kai to get his attention. "That was stupid, you dimwit. You're lucky Pop doesn't send your butt to shore after that stunt," he whispered.

Kai looked around, making sure no one was close enough to overhear. "That wasn't a stunt. I really fell."

Jack traded insults with Kai as they walked down the stairs to the cabin. He stopped at the sound of Val and Rachel cackling excitedly. Once inside, he understood as he took in the surrounding luxury. Nan walked over and put her arm around his waist. "*Reckless Endeavor* is a very pretty girl, but it's all about what's on the inside that counts." She added, with a sly grin, "I told Pop I'd love to sail, but preferred not to rough it."

Jack turned to face Nan. "This is a floating five-star hotel."

She shrugged. "Maybe four-star. Five-star would have gold-plated faucets."

The interior was finished with rich combinations of mahogany, leather, and highly polished brass. There were two staterooms, each with their own baths, two smaller bedrooms and separate crew quarters. The galley was outfitted with the latest in appliances. Special gimbals and borders were installed to keep cookware from shifting with the movement of the sea. In the salon, above a short but wide bookcase, the designer had mounted a big screen TV surrounded by sofas, chairs and tables, all fastened to the floor. Curiously, two rooms onboard remained locked and neither Pop nor Captain Sutton attempted to open them as part of the tour. Jack assumed one led to the engine room, the other to an unfinished storage space. He was only partly right.

"We'll take her for a little sail offshore today and get down to real business tomorrow. Sound like a plan, Captain Ron?"

"Aye, Captain Rackham."

~8~
SEA TRAILS

LAUGHIN' GAFF WAS POP'S high performance center console fishing boat. A thirty-eight-foot Donzi 38ZFX powered by three 300HP Mercury engines made it one of the fastest boats in the area. With the customized color scheme, electronics package and upgraded rigging systems, the craft made Pop look like a real pro on the water. He was pathetic at the sport of fishing, but as he said, he could always get home empty-handed faster than anyone else. Chewing on an unlit cigar, he sat in the swivel seat behind the helm of the boat with all engines running, waiting impatiently for Jack. They were meeting Captain Sutton for their first training session aboard *Reckless Endeavor.* The day was perfect.

Jack ran barefoot, down the dock, a deck shoe in each hand, and leaped aboard at the stern, and waited for the punctuality lecture that never came.

"Better get in your seat, I feel like crankin' up all nine hundred horsepower on this baby," said Pop as they moved from the dock. After a quick look all around, he pushed all three throttles forward to their stops.

They cruised north through the calm waters of the Matanzas at seventy miles per hour, slowing only a few times to avoid swamping smaller boats with their wake. Within ten minutes they were at trolling speed, traveling past the marina and under the Bridge of Lions. At its mooring in front of the Castillo de San Marcos, waited *Reckless Endeavor.* Jack hung the rubber fenders off the port side of *Laffin' Gaff.* They would set the bow anchor while Pop boarded the sailboat. Once Pop was aboard, Jack let *Laffin' Gaff* swing with the current and set the stern anchor, leaving him a short swim to the bigger boat.

Jack Rackham

Jack climbed the rope ladder, hopped over the gunwale and stood dripping wet facing Pop and the Captain. They seemed to be in the middle of a serious conversation when Jack interrupted. "We should have brought my boat so we could have tested out the davit and cradle."

"Ah, there's plenty of time for that. I wanted to give my boat a good run," said Pop.

Jack laughed. "You're not the one taking the early-morning swim. I should have given you my shoes to carry up here. They're soaked."

"That's the least of our worries. Apparently Captain Sutton's deckhands abandoned ship sometime last night," said Pop.

"Maybe they went into town and lost track of time," said Jack.

Captain Sutton shook his head. "No, they ditched us. All of their gear is gone. My regular crew cancelled out on the trip so I ended up bringing that pair on at the last minute. I paid them, and they ran off. "

"Well, I'm glad they're gone. That guy with the white streak in his hair was eavesdroppin' on me n' Deb yesterday. I think he was trouble," said Pop.

"That was Dawson. I had a bad feeling about him from the start but I was in a bind and had to hire him on. Being short-handed won't be a problem. We can still sail; it's just going to make my job of tutoring a little tougher. By the way, let's get rid of the Captain stuff, just call me Ron." He turned to address Jack with his hands on his hips. "So tell me, what's the first thing we've got to do?"

"Uh, start the engine and heave the mooring line?"

Pop shook his head, pretending to be disappointed in his grandson's answer. "Ron, may I explain to this chucklehead lubber what we do first?"

"By all means, please do."

Handing Jack a small pouch he said, "Hoist the colors!"

Jack unfolded the black flag with the Rackham emblem. The skull and crossed cutlasses soon flapped in the breeze, as Captain Sutton ordered engines started and lines away. *Reckless Endeavor* motored slowly toward the inlet with Pop at the wheel.

Kai and Val were driving on the beach with surfboards mounted on top of the Jeep's roll bars looking for the best spot to surf. "What do you think Rachel's doing today?" asked Val.

"Don't know. Jack's sailin' with Pop. She's probably hangin' out at the house."

"Think we should go over and pick her up?"

"It's okay with me but you could have suggested it before we made it to the beach."

"I'm tired and didn't think about it before. Shoot me why don't ya."

"You really like her."

"Yeah, she's cool."

Kai turned off at one of the beach ramps leading to A1A, the road to the Rackham's house. "Are you sure you're not just feeling sorry for her?"

"Sure I feel sorry for her, she's been through a lot of bad stuff, then I had to go and embarrass her in the parking lot at the Old Jail the other night. There's just something about her that's the real deal. She doesn't play up the hard times like she's looking for sympathy."

"What about Talia?"

Val frowned. "Why do we always get back to that question? Talia's got to get over the princess act. She's the one that changed plans at the last minute. Whatever happens, happens."

"Wait'll she finds out Pop won't rearrange the trip to suit her," laughed Kai.

"Geez…what's she gonna do when she hears Rachel's going to the islands with us?"

"She's gonna go ballistic n' Jack's gonna tell Talia to take a hike," said Kai.

"Think so?"

"Know so. He's a nice guy, but he won't take crap from anybody." Kai punched in the code at the gates and drove up to the house. They found Rachel sitting next to one of the waterfalls in the lanai talking to Nan. As usual, Nan had her camera trained on an exotic plant.

Val spoke up first. "Hi guys. We stopped by to see if Rachel wanted to go to the beach."

"The waves are kinda lousy today but we might catch a few decent rides," said Kai.

Rachel looked toward Nan and back to Val. "I think I'll pass."

"Really? C'mon, we want you to hang out with us," said Val.

"Why?" asked Rachel.

Nan was trying to stay out of the conversation, but Rachel's response puzzled her. She didn't want to interfere by prodding Rachel into anything. Val looked annoyed but Kai, as usual, was grinning.

"That's the dumbest answer ever," said Kai. "Only a nit-wit Yankee could come up with that."

"I didn't give you an answer."

"Exactly. If somebody invites you to do somethin' the answer's either yes or no. If we didn't want you around, we wouldn't invite your sorry butt. Your choice, no big deal to me," said Kai.

Rachel looked at Val. "Is he always this tactful?"

"Subtle as a sledgehammer," said Val with a sigh.

"Is it okay with you?" Rachel asked Nan.

"Of course it's okay. Go have fun."

Captain Sutton showed Jack how to unfurl the sails once *Reckless* reached the open sea. It was normally a ten-minute job for a three-man crew but Pop wanted Jack to do the work alone, with Sutton's guidance. He believed there was no better way to learn than to actually complete a task, even if it was difficult. It helped that Jack was a fast learner. In less than twenty minutes, they were sailing. Pop stepped from behind the wheel, allowing his grandson to take over.

"The kid's a natural," said Sutton as he leaned against the gunwale with his arms folded.

"Yeah, smart as whip that one. Gets his brains n' good looks from me," said Pop.

"When do you want a demonstration of the built-in special features?"

"Let's wait a few days 'til he gets the sailin' part down. I want him to be able to sail this thing by himself and be comfortable doin' it."

"That's a tall order for a sixteen-year-old. A boat this size should be crewed by at least three decent sailors."

Pop nodded in agreement. "By the time we put out to sea, everyone will be up to speed on the basics and experts on some of the specifics."

"When are you setting sail?"

"Not for a couple weeks."

"Have you decided on a destination?" asked Sutton.

"I've charted one course to the Bahamas, and another to Jamaica."

"Jamaica would be a much longer trip. Quite a step for a maiden voyage."

"It would be, but I was seriously thinkin' about sailin' into Port Royal and Rackham's Cay for the sake of family history. I ain't gettin' any younger, so I don't want to put that trip off too long," said Pop.

"I suggest delaying the Jamaica trip until later, but if you decide to make that sail, hug the northwest side of the Windward Passage and avoid Golfe de la Gonave. It may sound strange this being the twenty-first century, but that area off the tip of Haiti is full of pirates. It's a very dangerous place."

"I'll keep that in mind. I had no idea," said Pop. "By the way, your crew didn't see our special features did they?"

"No. They thought *Reckless* was just a floating condominium with sails being delivered to some fat cat with more money than brains. When we were under power, I was at the regular controls using only the smaller auxiliary engine. Your secret's safe. Everything's been locked down since before leaving port."

"Other than being referred to as a brainless fat cat, your answer's a big relief. I still don't like how the one guy was sneakin' around."

Rachel was in the back seat of Kai's yellow jeep for the second time that week. She couldn't even remember the last time she had hung out with kids her own age but she would make the effort to fit in. They drove onto the beach and pulled up to the bottom of a dune. Kai went to the back door of the Jeep and removed a small folding table, setting it up a few yards away. He took out a small grill, a cooler and a bag of charcoal.

Rachel watched as Kai sprayed lighter fluid onto a pile of charcoal. "What's all this?"

"Duh! It's a cookout. We always grill on the beach. Ya like shrimp?" asked Kai.

"Yeah, I guess so. You're allowed to cook down here too?"

Val was laughing. "Pretty cool huh? We do this all the time. His shrimp wraps are killer. Nice n' spicy. Wanna take the boards out while our personal chef does his thing?"

"Yeah, I'll see if I've forgotten everything you taught me."

"Kai, do you mind being lonely for awhile?"

"Nah, go ahead, knock yourselves out."

Rachel peeled off her white cover up, still burnt from her first beach day. Val grabbed the larger of the two boards. "You'll want to use sunscreen soon. Fifteen minutes is all it takes to burn. A couple weeks in the sun, you'll have a nice base and before you know it, you'll look like a real Floridian."

They paddled out beyond the shallows and laid flat on the boards resting their chins on their forearms waiting for the surf to pick up. After a few minutes, Val spoke. "I owe you an apology."

"About what?"

"The other night. I shouldn't have teased you when you and Jack pulled up to the Old Jail. I'm really sorry."

"It's okay. I'm over it. No hard feelings. Now I need to clear the air," said Rachel. "Just so you know, your friend Talia's got nothing to worry about. Jack is way out of my league."

Val sat up on the board and paddled closer. "What's that supposed to mean?"

"What?"

"Out of your league." Val looked irritated.

Rachel forced a laugh as she explained. "Come on Val, he's a nice guy and his family's amazing. The Rackham's are crazy rich and can buy anything they want. I mean, look at the house and the boats. If that weren't enough, Jack's totally... hot. All of those things put him way out of my league." She was now sitting cross-legged on the board facing Val.

Val paused before answering. "You're right. The Rackham's have lots of money. They also do lots of nice things for people without making a show of it. If you had never been to Jack's house, you'd never have known he was loaded. I've never seen him show off or act…"

"I'm not saying…"

"Let me finish," said Val. "The point is, everything you say is true but that doesn't mean you don't count or that you're out of his league. First of all, money's not important. Secondly, look at yourself. You're gorgeous. On a scale of one to ten you're an eight." Val laughed. "You'll be an eleven once you work on your tan and visit Reni over at Aveda One. She's the girl that takes care of Nan. Best in the whole salon."

"Well, thanks, I guess. It doesn't change the fact that I'm a nobody and have nobody."

"You're totally wrong," Val sighed. "You're somebody and, by my count, you have at least five people in your life right now. Maybe we're all new arrivals, but we all care."

"Why are you trying to be nice to me?" asked Rachel.

"The why question again."

"Yeah, the why question. Comes up a lot. As you say, to be clear, I'm not looking for sympathy or anyone's handouts and I'm not interested in stealing someone's boyfriend."

"Good. Again, *to be clear*, you won't get sympathy or handouts from any of us. The boyfriend thing is none of my business and, just so you know, I hope Jack dumps my friend Talia 'cause I don't think she's been very nice to him. In fact, she hasn't been nice to anyone for a long time. There, I said it, to you, not to Jack. As for your other question, as sick as it may sound, I'm nice to people I like, but if you don't loosen up and stop with the cynic crap, I'm probably not gonna like you for very long." Val fully expected Rachel to paddle away toward shore.

"You're okay Val. You should take a breath once in awhile during your lectures, but you're still okay. I'll work on my tan and try to loosen up. Understand one thing; all of this is like some kind of dream, even being friends with you and Kai. I'm afraid I'm gonna wake up and it'll all be gone. You'll all be gone."

Val wanted to cry, but Rachel had made it plain that she wanted no sympathy. "Let's get to the beach. I need the sunscreen."

~9~
TWIN CATS

⌐THEY SAILED TWENTY MILES DUE east from the St. Augustine inlet. It was day five of the training and sea trials and time for Jack to learn the secrets of *Reckless Endeavor.*

"Furl the sails fellas!" hollered Pop.

"Pop, I already know how to do that. It's mostly electronic anyway so why are we practicing that again?" complained Jack.

"Don't question the Captain. I want everything tightened up in ten minutes."

"Awww…this is nuts."

"Nine minutes."

Jack hustled through the chore. Captain Sutton pitched in as everything was strapped into place. The job was finished in less than eight minutes. Jack walked to the helm and snapped a smart salute toward Pop. "Mission accomplished, sir!" he barked.

Pop laughed at that. "Good. Now let me show you why we needed to do that."

"What's this *we* stuff? You're standing behind the wheel like the guy on the frozen fish sticks box. All that's missing is the goofy yellow hat."

"Follow me, Jackson. It's time to let you in on somethin' top secret." Pop made a right turn at the bottom of the wooden stairs and walked to the mystery room, his keys jingling in hand. He unlocked the door, turned and motioned to Jack to follow him inside. It seemed to happen all in one fluid motion. "Here's part one."

Jack poked his head into the room, and looked down. He stared at two spotless yellow engines, the size of small cars, separated by a tall rectangular fiberglass box. "Better tell me what I'm looking at, Pop."

"Twin Caterpillar 1825 diesel engines. They'll push this baby thirty five to forty knots per hour, depending on conditions, of course."

"That's about forty-something miles per hour!"

"Now let me show you part two," said Pop.

"Ron, would you please operate the mast controls while we go topside to watch?"

"No problem," said the Captain as he moved to a panel covered with switches.

Jack walked upstairs to the deck with Pop.

"Step back. The riggin's about to drop."

There was a loud mechanical hum from the stern and, after a few seconds, the ratlines collapsed to the deck. The yardarms spun upward, aligning with the masts, before retracting by half their length, and then lowered gently to a pair of deck-mounted cradles. The conversion was all-automatic. "The telescoping masts are made of heavy gauge aluminum, covered with a colored synthetic to make them look like oak," explained Pop.

A loud grinding noise erupted from the engine room below causing Jack to shuffle back toward the helm. "Now what's that racket?"

"We're drawing part of the keel up into that box that you saw between the engines while the props extend. The next sound you hear will be the trim tabs leveling out from below the transom. Those will give the boat greater stability at higher speed. The shorter keel is necessary for handling. If you'll pull those handles in the deck, the winch in the engine room will coil up the rigging and get it out of the way."

"This is amazing. Who dreamed all this up?"

"Hmmm…I wonder. It's the work of a real genius. Good lookin' fella, someone you know real well. Now let's check out the topside command center." Pop walked past Jack to the helm and pressed three buttons. The large mahogany wheel was slowly swallowed into the deck, replaced by a new helm, complete with a pair of throttles and a bank of computer screens.

"Got one more thing to show you." Once again they trudged downstairs. The door to the second mystery room was opened, revealing a duplicate command center with large flat screen monitors on three walls. "If we ever need to operate at speed from down here, we'll need a full helm, not just the autopilot station near the galley. Five hidden cameras mounted topside feed live images to these monitors. This is a little crowded and I prefer runnin' up top, but this'll do in an emergency. Now whaddya say we take *Reckless* for a spin n' see what she does under real power."

"I've got to ask, so don't get mad at me. If you wanted all this power, why didn't you just buy a motor yacht? Why a sailboat?" asked Jack.

"Camouflage."

"Huh?"

"Your ears clogged?"

"No. I just didn't get the camouflage answer."

"When we get back to the house, I'll show you the rest of my plan and tell you more details 'bout what I expect to find. The thing is; we gotta look like tourists, not treasure hunters. A regular motor yacht, one with the same amount of deck space and equipment as *Reckless* would look suspicious. This'll just look like we're sailin' and divin' for fun from an old restored schooner."

"Sailing? With a boat like mine sitting on the stern?"

"Camouflage."

"Here we go again. I thought you said we needed it to get into shallower water."

"That's true, partly 'cause I don't wanna run around in one of those inflatable Zodiacs, bad back you know. *Bad Latitude* will hide the primary purpose for the davit crane. If it can lift your boat, it can also haul up the loot and lower it below the deck, into the hidden compartment behind the engine room."

"You're sounding a little paranoid."

"Nan said the same thing the other day, but when you see the stockpile of gold we're about to claim, you'll understand my paranoia."

"All that's missing is a set of cannons."

"Wasn't allowed to have 'em."

"Nan said no cannons?"

Pop laughed. "Nah. I'm kiddin'."

"You mean we've *got* cannons?"

"No we don't have cannons. I never thought to add 'em."

"So now what?"

"Now we stop talkin' like a coupla old hens and crank this thing up. I'll give you first honors. Stay parallel with the coast and don't creep any closer than twenty miles. If you see anyone gettin' close, slow down. Tomorrow we'll get everyone up to speed on their part in sailing this tub and, after a few more practice runs, we'll pack our provisions and get underway."

The schooner handled beautifully through the three-foot swells at top speed. After two hours, they shut the engines down, and hoisted the masts into place before unfurling the sails for the trip to port. The transformation from full power to sail took twenty minutes, double the time it had taken to go from sail to power. An hour later, they sailed into the Matanzas toward the Castillo.

"Tomorrow let's bring your boat and set it in the cradle and see how she handles."

"I thought you said we were all sailing for the next few days."

"We are."

"So you're gonna let everyone in on the secret?"

"No, we're just sailin'. Don't breathe a word about those engines to anyone, 'specially Kai. He finds out, so will half of St. Augustine," said Pop as Captain Sutton tied the schooner off at its mooring.

It was late afternoon when Jack walked through the double doors into Pop's study. The walls were lined with mahogany shelves stuffed with expensive books. In the corner stood a century-old binnacle covering a polished brass compass. Pop's desk, made from the salvaged helm of a sunken ship, was nearly twelve feet wide; the top protected by a single sheet of thick beveled glass. It was centered in front of a pair of French doors, which opened to a small balcony overlooking the inland waterway. The wall space not taken up with bookshelves was covered with a collection of fine paintings of historic sailing scenes from the nineteenth century alongside ancient maps, all displayed within ornate gilded frames. The chairs and sofas were deep red leather, with shiny brass tacking at the edges. It was the only dark room in the entire house, resembling a well-appointed drawing room from a stodgy Victorian-Era yacht club. He was standing at the credenza inspecting a framed family photo when Pop arrived.

"You remember that?" asked Pop.

It was a picture of Jack at two-years-old, wearing a tiny orange and blue life jacket, concentrating intently as he gripped the stainless steering wheel of one of Pop's early boats. His curly blonde hair blew backwards toward Pop, who was firmly stationed behind, holding his grandson in position at the helm. A wide frothy blue-white wake trailed in the background. "Where did this come from? I've never seen this picture before in my life."

"You really don't remember that?"

"No. I was what…two or three?"

"Not quite two. It was the first time you'd ever handled a boat."

"You mean I was steering?"

"Yep. Did a great job as I recall."

"Where was this taken?"

"Indian River Bay in Longneck, Delaware. Me n' Nan had a little beach house there. That was my third boat and your very first ride. We sold that place when you turned three."

"Look at you with the doo rag and tattoos. Your hair was long and your beard was blonde."

"Yeah, not much gray in it in those days, but it's all white now. A guy really goes downhill in fourteen years."

"Nan looks pretty much the same as her pictures from back then."

"She pay you to say that?"

Jack laughed. "Time to change the subject."

"You're smarter than you look." Pop walked toward the drawing table, giving Jack the *follow me* sign. "I bought these copper discs a few years back up in North Carolina. They're rumored to have belonged to Calico Jack Rackham and Anne Bonny. These were their version of treasure maps. Stay with me now, it gets complicated. When I place them on this chart with the arrow pointing north, these numbers match up with the latitudes on the map. Counting backwards, by the same number leads to an arrow with the line etched starting from this tiny little sun. Ignore all the lines 'cept the one with the sun."

"Okay, I see it."

"Now I'll do the same with this disc. See? It's the same set point, but the arrow points to a different island. Third one's the same."

"That doesn't narrow it down very well."

"See these marks? They're just like ones you would find on an engineer's scale. These are measurements."

"How do you know that?"

"I looked up documents on how mapmakers did their surveys. The only thing I can't figure out is the single numeral on the opposite side of the plate. This one is marked with a seven; the others are engraved with a five and a three. Maybe there were more discs and stockpiles of treasure so they numbered 'em to keep track. I think I've figured out how they work, it's a triangulation trick."

"Maybe it's another code."

"Hope not. That would screw up all my calculations."

"What do you think we'll find, Pop?"

"Only the treasure of a lifetime." Pop tapped his fingers absently on the chart. "On this trip, we're only searchin' one island, the one where I think the biggest Rackham stash is hidden. He captured a ship sailing from Central America bound for Spain with a bellyful of Aztec gold, that's all a matter of record. Problem was, his boat was smaller than the Spaniard's and couldn't handle the weight. He had to offload it close by so his own ship wouldn't sink. Based on my triangulation theory using the discs; it seems to make sense to look here." Pop drew a squiggly circle around the unnamed island with a red felt-tipped pen.

"Guess we'll see how your detective work turns out."

"Could be a total waste of time."

"Nah. Even if we don't find anything, this trip's gonna be cool."

Pop sat down behind the desk and propped his feet on the corner and let out a long sigh. "It'd be nice to find at least enough to cover the cost of the boat. Nan's callin' it my floatin' money pit."

"So did you and Nan decide …"

"You mean will Nan and the girls stay aboard while we look for the loot?"

"Yeah."

"No. We're gonna take our time, kinda like a vacation. Make some stops along the way, do some divin' and such. After that, Nan and the girls are gonna stay with some friends at a nice place on Grand Bahama. They'll have a great time, and you know Nan's gonna spoil Rachel and Val rotten the whole time."

"What's Rachel think about this excursion?"

"She's goin' is all I know. I haven't talked to her much these last few days 'cause I've been busy gettin' ready for the trip. Now that you mention it, wonder what she's been up to?"

"Kai and Val were teaching her how to snorkel and dive."

"Around here?"

"In the pool."

"Snorkelin's okay, but she's not gonna learn how to use tanks and regulators and all the safety stuff in time for divin' on this trip."

"She learned to surf in one day."

"Big difference."

"Maybe she can dive in the shallower water."

"That's fine, but I don't want her divin' any of those blue holes."

"I don't know if I want to dive them. It's too easy to get trapped." Jack stared at the chart.

Pop laughed. "You'll dive 'em. One look and you won't be able to resist."

~10~
SHIPSHAPE

~THEY DOCKED RECKLESS ACROSS the end of St. Augustine's municipal pier to load and pack the equipment and provisions. Captain Sutton, the proud owner of a very fat check covering final payment for his hard work, had taken an early flight to Rhode Island the day before. Pop hired a private security company to keep curious locals and tourists from boarding the boat. Nan still believed Pop to be paranoid.

Jack and Kai were sitting at the stern when Pop walked up the gangplank carrying a waterproof case. "You guys have all the stuff packed away?"

"Yep. Everything's shipshape. All we have left to do is load the girls' suitcases as soon as we get the word," said Jack.

"Good. We'll get that done this afternoon."

Kai laughed. "There he goes with that *we* stuff. Hasn't carried a thing on board 'cept that case he's holdin'."

"I heard that. You guys will hafta use my truck to haul their stuff. Knowin' Nan, she's probably packed enough for six months at sea wearin' three outfits a day," grumped Pop.

"Who's gonna feed quarters in the parkin' meter while we're gone?" teased Kai.

"You are, if you don't stop pickin' on me," said Pop. "Now listen up. You two chuckleheads are gonna drop everyone off at the dock in the mornin', then go back n' get Jack's boat. Once we get *Bad Latitude* hoisted into the cradle, we're gonna shove off. Gotta be efficient."

"What time do you think we'll be underway?" asked Jack.

"Let's see…we're scheduled to leave around eight, I told Nan seven. Factor in three females, make-up, gettin' the hair just right… I'd say ten, maybe eleven."

"So what's in the case?" asked Kai.

"Wouldn't you like to know."

"Is it chained to your wrist?"

"Very funny. This is our ticket boys. The keys to the Rackham treasure. We find this baby, I'll be able to retire," answered Pop as he glanced at Jack.

"You've been retired for years," said Jack.

"Semi-retired. This time it'll be for good. Just gonna relax."

Jack grinned at Kai before turning again to face Pop. "So what's our percentage of the take gonna be?"

"Depends. I have a formula all figured out. Your shares go up if you have any close calls…or lose any limbs. It's kinda like the way pirates divvied things up. If you get a leg chopped off or somethin' you get an extra quarter percent. How's that sound?"

"Sounds like there's gonna be a mutiny," laughed Kai. "Hey, has anyone ever retired before they graduated from high school?"

"I dunno, but if there's as much loot as I think there is, you guys, your kids n' your grandkids will be set for life. I'd better get this thing locked away in the safe," said Pop as he started down the steps to the stateroom.

Rachel was in the guest room, the one everyone now referred to as *Rachel's room*, sorting through the new clothes and bathing suits, packing everything for the trip into two large suitcases. Rummaging through the closet, she noticed her frayed beige bag, tucked neatly on a corner shelf next to her old clothes. Everything was clean and folded. Her eyes filled as she thought about how her circumstances had turned around so completely in such a short time.

It was complicated. She didn't belong. From that very first morning, the Rackham's had treated her like part of their family, but it didn't change the fact that her parents were dead and she had no one. Val and Kai were friendly and genuine enough, and she enjoyed their company. They made her laugh and convinced her to try new things. Jack, on the other hand, was a problem. He had been her hero from the start, and she had expected, once sympathy for the poor homeless girl had diminished, that he would turn into the privileged conceited type, making her feel like a debt was somehow owed. It never happened. If anything, he was friendlier and more attentive than ever, in a good kind of way. Her face reddened as she remembered their boat ride. Something had clicked. It had given her butterflies and made her head swim, a good but scary feeling. She'd seen his embarrassment when he had compared the color of her eyes to the sea; he had let his guard down. A smile formed as the moment flooded her memory.

They would set sail early in the morning. How was she going to survive the trip, pretending he was just *some guy*? She was crazy about him and couldn't get him out of her thoughts. Nan knew. So did Val. That was another problem. She stared at the tattered bag and the small stack of clothes. It would take only a few minutes to pack and leave a note. It would be for the best, for everyone. Rachel picked up the bag, the one memento from her street life, and cried.

She heard Nan climbing the staircase and hurried into the bathroom, closed the door and turned on the faucet. She washed her face with a cloth to hide the signs of her closet cry, and tied her hair back before returning to the bedroom. Nan was down the hall poking through the shelves of a linen closet as Rachel resumed packing. As she zipped the larger of the two bags, Nan entered the room.

"If you're at all uncomfortable about making this trip, let me know, Rachel. I'm sure the boys would manage just fine if we stayed behind." Nan looked concerned.

"I'm okay. I wouldn't want to ruin your plans."

"My priority is helping you sort things out. I want to make sure that you're okay. There's no reason for you to do something you don't want to do."

"Really, Nan, I'm fine. A little nervous, but fine," answered Rachel making a weak attempt to smile.

"He wants you to go, in case you hadn't noticed."

"What do you mean?"

"Jack's excited that you're going on the trip. Rachel, you really need to be more observant."

Rachel lowered her head. "He barely knows I'm alive."

Nan laughed out loud. "If that's the case, he has an odd way of showing it. Look, I'm not suggesting any happily ever after stuff, that's a rarity among sixteen-year-olds, but do yourself a favor and let your guard down a little. Enjoy the summer. Don't worry about what anyone thinks, including me. Do what makes you happy," said Nan as she gave Rachel a quick shoulder hug.

"You really think he, uh, kinda likes me?"

"Well, I'm not going to get into Jack's business, but I'll let you in on a secret, if he doesn't like someone, they'll know it and they'll know it right away. He's like Pop that way, not very good at hiding stuff like that." Nan walked toward the doorway of the bedroom and turned around. "One other thing I should mention; we all want you to be part of the family. If you decide to leave, we won't try to talk you out of it, but I would be really upset if I was to find that beat up old bag missing from the closet." With that, she left the room leaving Rachel to wonder if Nan had known what she had been thinking all along.

Rachel zipped up the second bag and wheeled it next to the first in time to hear Jack walk in from the back porch. He and Kai were jabbering away at one another as usual, as Nan intercepted them.

"What are you two doing here already? I thought we'd have a couple more hours of peace and quiet," teased Nan.

"We're ready to load your stuff. Got a moving van on the way, should be here any minute," said Jack with a smirk.

"Moving van? We're not bringing *that* much."

"Whaddya bringin' ten or twelve suitcases each?" asked Kai.

"Two each," answered Nan. "We're going to shop for the rest of what we need when we get to Grand Bahama."

"Boat's gonna be pretty well loaded down for the return trip. Won't be much room for a bunch of frilly clothes," said Jack.

"Then we'll have to fly back," quipped Nan. "Jack are you all packed or did you just show up early to annoy me?"

"Take me two seconds. Toothbrush and iPhone and I'm good to go."

"You're wearing the same shorts and underwear for a whole month?"

"Same shorts, no underwear," said Jack. He heard Rachel giggle from the other side of the room and felt his face redden.

"No shoes, no shirt, no problems," interrupted Kai. "We're not even gonna shave for the whole trip. The grubbier n' stinkier the better. Like pirates."

"Well I don't expect anyone will notice the beards but no one's wearing the same dirty clothes on that boat for a whole month. Now go get packed," ordered Nan.

"Can't right now."

"Why not?"

"Too hungry. Lack of energy. Lightheaded n' stuff."

Nan shook her head. "So you'll pack fresh underwear if I feed you, is that the deal?"

"Pretty much," said Jack.

"Okay, you pack and I'll see what I can scrounge together. There's not much here you know." Nan smiled at Rachel as the boys bolted through the back door toward the boathouse. "Thinks he's funny, that duffle bag of his has been packed for a week."

Nan and Rachel were sitting at the table when Jack and Kai returned ten minutes later. Jack inhaled deeply through his nose. "Ah, something smells really good."

"Maryland crab cakes. Boys, your lunch is on the bar. Are the crab cakes good Rachel? No shells I hope," said Nan.

Kai rubbed his hands together as they walked toward the kitchen breakfast bar. "What's this stuff?" asked Jack.

"Sardines, in a can. Just pull the tab back, but don't spill that nasty fish oil on your clothes."

"Whoa dude. She dogged us," whispered Kai. "Looks like bait."

Rachel plastered her hand across her mouth to stifle a laugh. Nan was pretending to ignore Jack while enjoying her crab cake, but the smiling eyes gave her away.

"C'mon, Kai," said Jack, "I'm gonna go unpack."

"Are you saying you don't like sardines?" asked Nan.

"I think they're great. Not as good as crab cakes and not worth having to pack clean clothes."

Nan sighed. "Alright, you two, forget the sardines." She took the cover off a dish in the center of the table. It was stacked with crab cakes surrounding a mound of potato salad. Rachel reached over and uncovered the plates and silverware hidden beneath the tablecloth. Jack and Kai jumped into their seats grinning as the back door slammed.

"I'm late, sorry. Are the crab cakes gone?" asked Val as she hurried into the kitchen.

Kai elbowed Jack as Nan and Rachel shared a laugh. "We were set up, amigo."

Jack squinted at Nan with one eyebrow raised, before turning to Rachel. "We'll get even. We always do."

Val was puzzled. "What's goin' on? What did I miss?"

Kai waved his hand. "It's a long story. All started 'cause Jack doesn't want to wear underwear."

"Geez, sorry I asked," said Val as she helped herself to lunch.

‍11‍
THE BERMUDA TRIANGLE

THE DAVIT WORKED PERFECTLY as it hoisted *Bad Latitude* into the cradle at the stern with no sign of strain. A crowd gathered at the dock to watch as the crew of teenagers prepared *Reckless Endeavor* for the voyage. Pop stood at the wheel with the engine running as the dock master loosened the spring line and tossed it to Jack waiting onboard. With barely a sound, the schooner pulled slowly from the wharf and turned toward the center of the Bridge of Lions. After three short blasts of the horn, the crossing arms on the bridge swung downward to block traffic, accompanied by warning bells and red blinking lights. The center span of the bridge opened upward in a slow yawn, allowing room for the masts to clear as Pop navigated the sailboat through its opening. Drivers waiting on the bridge abandoned their vehicles to watch and wave as *Reckless* crossed to the inlet side of the span, others blew their horns offering a 'thumbs up' from their open windows while Nan, Val and Rachel returned their waves from the deck below. One long blast of the horn from Pop signaled the all clear and the massive grates folded together restoring the roadway As soon as they cleared the bridge, Pop ordered all sails unfurled. The vessel dwarfed the surrounding boats that had formed up in a kind of escort pattern cruising alongside and behind toward the inlet. The billowing white sails stood out in stark contrast against the calm jade-green waters of the bay and the cloudless blue skies, creating a majestic spectacle. They were on their way.

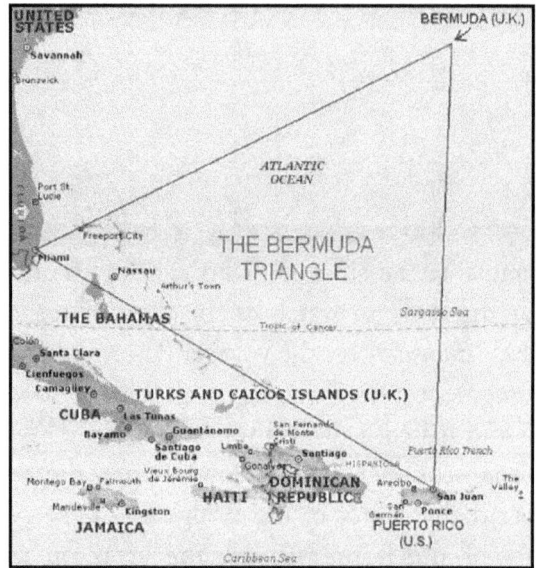

The Bermuda Triangle

Nan moved next to Pop at the helm. "So much for a low key exit."

"Yeah. How 'bout that? It was like we had a private *bon voyage* party."

"Of course, unfurling the sails didn't help draw much attention," said Nan.

"Well, I wanted to… you know…" Pop was groping for words.

"I think the term is *show off*," offered Nan.

"Maybe a little," said Pop with a grin. "She's a beauty though ain't she?"

"Sure is nicer than that fourteen foot aluminum skiff we started out with."

"We had some good times on that boat. Haven't lake-fished since we sold it."

"I out-fished you in those days too," said Nan as she patted Pop on the back. "Remember all of those bass I caught at Marsh Creek State Park?"

"Okay, rub it in. We're still close enough to shore for you to swim back."

"All bark no bite." Nan gave Pop a peck on the cheek and turned to leave. "I'm going below to change."

"Already? We're not even a mile out."

"You just drive the boat."

"Aye aye, Cap'n," said Pop.

"Wanna climb the rat lines to the top of the mast?" asked Kai. "It'll be a nice view."

"Don't think so," said Val absently as she stared at the chart glowing from the computer screen. "Did you know we're sailing through the Bermuda Triangle?"

"Yeah, sometimes people call it The Devil's Triangle. What about it?"

Rachel perked up and looked at Jack. "Isn't that where ships and planes disappear without a trace?"

"There are stories and legends about it, but no proof. I think it's all hype. Ships sink and planes crash, usually from weather problems or piloting mistakes. The forecast is for light winds and calm seas, and we have the latest navigational equipment and gadgetry onboard. We'll be fine," said Jack. Val and Rachel didn't look convinced.

"When will we actually be in the Triangle?" asked Val.

"Probably two days from now. It's only a name for an area on the map that goes from Miami to Bermuda, Bermuda to Puerto Rico and Puerto Rico to Miami, making a triangle. Nothing but a bunch of old sailor tales," answered Jack.

"Well I've heard that compasses and electronics don't always work when you're inside the thing. People believe there are big holes in the ocean that just suck planes and ships to the bottom," argued Val.

Kai snickered. "You watch too much Discovery Channel. Guess you believe in Bigfoot, The Turner Beast and The Loch Ness Monster too."

"I didn't believe in ghosts before last summer and you know how that turned out."

"Okay, good point." Kai stood and walked toward the main mast.

"Where are you goin'?" asked Val.

"Up top. I gotta keep an eye out for Nessy or maybe a giant boat-eating squid or maybe white whales. Think we're safe from Bigfoot though. Not much of a saltwater guy I hear."

"He's nuts," said Val. "Guess I'll climb up n' see what the view's like."

"They're both crazy," said Rachel as she stared upward. "The Turner Beast is real, by the way. It stalks the woods in Maine near my...old house."

"Do you miss Maine?" asked Jack.

"With my parents both gone, not really. I know I'm not gonna miss the cold. It was a nice place, don't get me wrong, but I had to get away from the bad memories." Rachel's curiosity got the better of her and she stumbled on. "How about you? You ever miss anything?"

"No."

"Nothing at all?"

"Nothing at all." Jack stared off trance-like at the incoming rollers feeling the boat rise and fall and thought about Talia. Neither had called or texted one another. Soon *Reckless* would be out of range for cell phones and text messages, which was fine by him. "Absolutely nothing at all," he repeated, with just the faint hint of a smile. "Wanna climb up top?"

"I'm afraid of heights."

"Time to face your fears." Jack reached out and tugged her by the hand. "Let's go."

Two days running under sail at a comfortable seven knots and everything worked as if scripted. It was nearly midnight and Pop, stationed behind the helm, puffed contentedly on a Romeo Y Juliette cigar under a brilliant canopy of stars. Nan and the girls had retired to their beds, while Kai relaxed playing a video game. Jack shuffled topside carrying Pop's light jacket over one arm and a cup of coffee in each hand. "Thought you could use these," he said handing over a ceramic mug with the Rackham logo plastered on its side.

"Thanks, Jackman. It's gettin' a bit nippy out here. Doesn't get better n' this does it kid?"

"Don't suppose it does Pop."

"Tomorrow we'll hit one of the out islands off Grand Bahama. I think we'll anchor there for a few days and do some divin' and fishin', whaddya think?"

"Sounds good to me. I'll set up the outriggers on *Bad Latitude* in the morning," said Jack.

"Be nice to get a marlin on the line."

"Mahi would be even better. I doubt that we could get a marlin in my boat."

"Ah, I wouldn't wanna bring it on board. Just get it alongside the boat n' take pictures. My friends wouldn't believe it without…"

"Pop, what's that on the radar?"

Pop leaned forward squinting at the screen. He reached inside the console, removed a pair of rimless glasses and leaned forward toward the screen again. "It's too big to be another vessel."

"Looks like it's moving this way in a big hurry if I'm reading this right," said Jack.

"Yeah, I don't like it one bit either. Must be some kind of heavy squall or a tropical depression."

"Can't be Pop. It just showed up while I was standing here. Tropical depressions form pretty slow and from further east."

"Okay let's change course fifteen degrees n' furl the sails. The way it's movin' it'll be on top of us in half an hour or so. Get Kai up here so we can get situated."

"Think we should drop the masts and switch over to the CAT engines, you know, in case we have to outrun whatever it is?"

Pop massaged his goatee and sighed before looking at the screen again. "Look at this. We altered course and so did… whatever's out there. Yeah, let's change over to the CATs. Wake everyone below n' tell 'em to get life jackets on and give us a hand. Throw a couple more straps on your boat & let's get the decks cleared. Hurry up, it's gainin' speed."

Jack bolted through the doors into the salon to warn everyone. Pop started the winches to furl the sails. He couldn't run the big engines while the deep keel and masts were in place. It was a safety feature built-in to prevent the mistake of running top heavy. The total transformation would take ten minutes, if all went smoothly.

Nan followed Jack and Kai to the deck on the run. The seas churned and the winds picked up, edging toward a gale force. Pop pointed at the screen, shouting above the building noise, he explained the predicament to Nan. Val and Rachel clambered through the doorway as the last sail was secured. Both fumbled awkwardly with the straps of their life jackets. Jack ran over to help.

"We've got something headed this way and you're going to hear lots of noise. It's probably going to be a really rough ride so I want both of you to go below and make sure there's nothing loose or lying around that could turn into a projectile." Jack pulled the straps tight and double-checked that the jackets were snug.

"Are we in the Bermuda Triangle now?" asked Val.

"Yes, since early this morning."

"So this is how ships disappear," said Rachel matter-of-factly.

"No. This is a tropical storm or something. Forget the Triangle stuff."

Kai ratcheted the last strap on *Bad Latitude* as Pop yelled above the wind for everyone to stand back. A moment later the rigging let loose and thundered to the deck.

"Oh crap! We're dead in the water now. What're we gonna do…" Kai stopped at mid-sentence as he stared upward to watch the yardarms move into their vertical positions aligning with the masts. "What the h…"

"I'll explain later," said Jack. "Open that hatch and pull those levers while I feed the rigging. There's a winch below that'll coil them up. When the brass hooks reach you, snap them into the eyelets inside."

The girls secured things below. They bounced from side to side as *Reckless* crashed through the fifteen-foot waves. Nan steadied herself against the frame of the stairway. "Okay girls, let's grab the emergency kits and get them topside. They're in the engine room. We'll see what Pop wants us to do after that," she said calmly. If Nan was scared, she didn't show it and her tone gave nothing away.

The tempest was building. Pop worried that the battering motion of the seas would twist the masts on the way down, making it impossible to secure them to the deck. He second-guessed his safety measures now, realizing that they would be nothing more than a useless floating hull without the CAT engines. Kai shimmied his way to the top of each partially retracted mast and looped nylon ropes around the ends with slipknots. Jack shook his head at his acrobatic friend as Kai rappelled effortlessly to the deck while *Reckless* listed violently from side to side. Pop hung onto the wheel to keep the rudder under control. The red mass on the radar screen was nearly on top of them and still they had no clue what it could be. The pattern did not resemble any storm he had ever seen as an expanding shape, a triangle, opened near the center. Finally, Kai and Jack managed to guide the masts into the security brackets and tightened the quick-lock bolts while *Reckless*, bobbed helplessly in the treacherous seas that crashed over the gunwales and across the bow. Jack skidded against the wheelhouse giving Pop the *all clear* to raise the keel and start the engines.

The radar showed the red blotch on the screen slide over their position. Pop flipped the ignition switches and the twin CATs roared to life. Kai crawled on all fours to join Jack. Waves towered above the schooner, now reaching a height of thirty feet. Nan opened the door to the salon and shoved the emergency kits onto the deck. Pop motioned to Jack and yelled above the gale, "Secure them at the stern next to the in-flatable lifeboat. Kai, get below and tell them to huddle up on the floor. Grab the headsets n' give me n' Jack a pair. If we need to abandon ship, I'll give you the word and you help the girls get out."

"Abandon ship?" yelled Kai.

"We gotta be prepared for anything. Go on. Go!"

Kai handed the communication headsets to Jack through the salon door. He stumbled down the stairs while strapping his own headset into place and adjusting the mike. "Pop said for you guys to huddle up here on the floor in case we need to…uh…go up top."

"You mean in case we have to jump overboard," said a teary-eyed Val.

"We'll be fine," said Nan. "Kai, tell Pop that I think he and Jack should run the boat from the helm down here so they don't get washed overboard."

"What other helm?"

"It's the one next to the engine room. You don't know about that?"

"There's a lot of stuff on this boat that I don't know about," said Kai.

Kai keyed the mic and passed along the message before turning toward Nan. "Pop says he and Jack are strapped in. They need to stay up there to keep an eye on the radar and the waves. The screen down here is too …" Nan started to say something but Kai held up his finger. Pop was on the radio barking in his ear. "He says he has to stay up there so he knows when to speed up or slow down with the way the waves are breaking."

Nan shook her head and reached for the headset when Kai spoke again. "He said for you to leave the headset alone and for me to get in the other control room and switch over to channel sixteen…and he wants the big floodlights flipped on at the bow. Says you know where the switch is."

"Come on, I'll show you," said Nan as she swayed ahead toward the engine room.

Rachel looked over at Val and smiled weakly. "Does anything faze these people?"

Val, her face pallid, laughed nervously. "Nothin.' Might as well get used to it. One of these days, I'll fill you in."

"If we get out of this mess, I guess this'll be the last boat ride we ever take," said Rachel.

"We'll get out of it okay. The Rackham's might be a little crazy, but they know what they're doing. If anybody can get through this storm it's them."

Rachel paused. "What if it's not just a storm? What if it *is* the Bermuda Triangle trying to get us?"

Nan overheard part of the conversation as she crawled on all fours into the room. She smiled as she collapsed onto the floor between the two girls and turned to face Rachel. "If it *is* the Bermuda Triangle sweetie, my money's still on the Rackham boys up there. Everything's going to be fine. Just think of this as a Jack Rackham adventure."

Reckless shuddered violently and rolled hard to port. Glass shattered in the galley and furniture smashed against the walls. The timbers of the schooner strained against the crushing weight of the seawater. Several seconds passed before *Reckless* righted herself.

The wind blew the tops off the angry whitecaps as the seas churned. *Reckless* labored forward crashing against towering walls of white water. Pop worked the throttles feverishly, speeding up to climb on the rise, holding back on the drops, trying to slide down rather than tumble helplessly down the reverse side of each of the deadly monsters. As Pop controlled speed, Jack fought the wheel, trying to prevent the schooner from twisting beam to sea. A broadside hit would capsize the vessel and she would become another *Triangle* statistic. His broad shoulders knotted into painful spasms while his forearms and biceps throbbed from the unrelenting pressure of the sea against the rudder, which forced the wheel to fight against his every correction. Jack was sure his vice-like grip would snap the wheel or rip it from the helm's frame but he continued the battle, leaning into each turn even harder as the salt water stung his eyes and burned his lungs. Thankfully, Pop had stubbornly insisted they wear harnesses and clip themselves to the deck-mounted stainless steel eyehooks to keep from washing overboard. Looking ahead toward the next bank of waves Jack noticed stars flickering across a brilliant night sky while the moon, looking much like a fingernail, floated high overhead. He wondered if the lack of driving rain and searing lightning, common partners with gusting winds and high seas, was one of nature's oddities or perhaps there was something more sinister at work. Maybe the legends of the Bermuda Triangle had some merit after all.

Pop checked the radar screen once more. "That mass, whatever it is, is almost on top of us."

"Hurricane?" asked Jack.

"Can't be. There was nothing in the forecast for that. Call down n' see if Kai's hearin' anything on the radio. Tell 'im to check NOAA, see if we're dealin' with a tropical storm or… whatever."

"You'd better get him on the horn, I got my hands full of this wheel," hollered Jack into the lip mike.

"Sorry. Wasn't thinkin'. You holdin' up okay? Need a break?"

"I'm okay," Jack lied.

Pop nodded, switched channels and spoke with Kai. A couple minutes passed before Pop relayed Kai's report that no storms were being tracked, no distress signals had been called in from other vessels, and there was nothing unusual on the NOAA band. In fact, Kai had attempted three times to radio their position and describe their problem to the Bahamas Air Sea Rescue. BASR had promptly reminded Kai that it was illegal to make false reports and clicked off when he tried explaining their predicament further. It wasn't necessary for Pop to mention that their chances of survival were looking grim at best. He looked at Jack with a smirk and nodded forward with his chin, one eyebrow arched. "Think we can make this one, Jackman?"

Jack's heart sank as he stared into the face of a ninety-foot wave climbing upward off the bow. As they reached its base, Pop took a deep breath and pushed both throttles to their limits spreading his feet apart as if that would somehow help coax more horsepower from the powerful CAT engines. Their survival would come down to power and timing.

"Keep her straight, 'specially on the back slope. She'll flip n' roll if the stern twists," yelled Pop over the headset. "When we get within half a boat length of the trough, tweak her starboard just a tad so she won't plunge nose first underwater."

"Got it. A tweak and a tad. Sounds like a plan," yelled Jack.

Reckless climbed. Jack held her steady as they neared the top. If Pop throttled back too late, the boat would tumble forward and control would be lost, causing them to plunge bow first into the depths on the opposite side. Too soon and she'd be whipped backwards with the cresting wave, crushed and splintered under millions of gallons of foaming seawater. It would be the ultimate test of seamanship and pure nerve. The schooner was nearing vertical. Jack, like Pop, widened his stance, angling hard against the supports of the helm seats. Once the boat tipped forward, he would have to maintain his balance and adjust his feet to take his weight off the wheel or risk over-steering and losing control. His reaction time would be limited to a blink.

Kai crashed backwards through the door of the engine room. He barely managed to hook his leg around the steel stair stringer before bashing his head into one of the twin diesels. The smell of fuel and burning rubber was pungent as he dangled upside down. Grabbing the open tread, he pulled himself through the opening into the hallway of the salon and crawled forward toward Nan and the girls. All of them were lying flat trying to hang on as *Reckless* continued the steep climb. Winded by the time he reached them, he leaned up in a semi-sitting position and shouted above the crashing sounds of furniture thrashing around the cabin. "Roll next to the steps and curl up with your feet facing the bow. We're gonna top this wave and goin' down's gonna be as steep as it is goin' up. Hurry or we'll crash headfirst!" They did as Kai ordered an instant before he stretched himself sideways below their feet. He jammed his heels against the inside of a door frame and wrapped one arm through the bottom section of the brass rail at the foot of the stairs as *Reckless* seemed to level out slightly. Rachel screamed as the boat plunged downward. Kai grabbed the rail awkwardly with his other hand holding on, using his body as a barricade to keep Nan, Val and Rachel from plummeting downward toward the bow.

Pop pulled back hard on both throttles at the very moment the bow dipped downward, beyond the wave's apex. Jack's concentration was total as he battled to keep the boat from fishtailing through the plunge. The high-powered spotlights cut through the salty gloom enough to help him focus on a landing point. The sea erupted with an explosion of white water as they landed perfectly into the face of an oncoming roller. Pop throttled one-third ahead as *Reckless* rose from the shallow trough. It took several seconds before realizing they had conquered the final wave. The seas ahead were calm, the wind reduced to a balmy breeze. Wordlessly, Pop reduced speed and unhooked his harness. He staggered to the cabin door and limped down the steps to check on everyone below. Jack scanned the horizon for signs of rogue waves before removing his own harness. As he reached the entrance to the cabin, Kai climbed onto the deck.

"Everybody okay down there?" asked Jack.

"Yeah. Shook up, maybe a few bruises, nothin' serious," said Kai.

"Man that was one wild ride. I thought we'd bought it for sure," said Jack as he stretched his arms behind his back to loosen his knotted muscles. "Glad that's over."

Kai gazed across the stern and let out a deep sigh. "I think we only survived round one. Round two is heading this way."

"What are you talking about?"

"Look behind us. Ever see anything like that?"

Jack moved next to Kai to see for himself. His shoulders slumped. "No way."

"Yes way. It's headed right for us and it's suckin' us backwards," said Kai.

"Tell everyone to hang on," said Jack as he returned to the helm. He didn't wait for Kai to get down the steps before jamming the throttles forward, all the way to their stops. The CAT engines rumbled as *Reckless* lurched forward, pushing the boat away from the swirling beams of light that spiraled upward from below the sea. Jack watched the whirlpool form as it pulled against the boat's frothy wake making it part of a wide circular current.

Pop and Kai returned to the deck. They heard the strange noise over the sound of the engines, air mixing with water, like a giant bathtub draining. The beam of light spread as the whirlpool grew and the spinning water behind gained speed. Jack felt *Reckless* bog down against the backward pull. Pop yelled over the horrific noise. "Take her forty-five degrees southeast n' use the spin to pick up some speed 'stead of fightin' it." He turned toward Kai. "We gotta dump Jack's boat. That's five thousand pounds we can't be draggin'. Cut the straps n' I'll swing the davit."

"You want to abandon *Bad Latitude*?" asked Kai.

"No choice," said Pop.

Jack nodded. "He's right Kai. Got to cut her loose or we'll have no shot."

"I can't believe I'm doin' this," yelled Kai as he ran toward Jack's boat. "This sucks."

Kai climbed aboard and slashed at the straps with his dive knife. He worked feverishly, while his mind replayed the memories of the previous summer's adventures aboard *Bad Latitude*. His stomach ached as he dropped the last strap and climbed over the fiberglass gunwale, giving Pop the all clear signal as he finished the chore. He clutched the black rope, tied off at *Bad Latitude's* stern cleat, pulling back to keep the twenty-two foot boat from spinning and smashing against *Reckless.* The davit whirred, easily lifting the heavy load before its arm swung out over the water, leaving Jack's gleaming blue and white boat to dangle above the waves. Kai kept steady pressure on the tag line, waiting for the boat to hit the water. After several seconds, he peeked over his shoulder and noticed Jack concentrating on the horizon ahead of *Reckless,* determined not to watch *Bad Latitude* set adrift and swallowed by the whirlpool. Given the all ready from Pop, Jack slowed *Reckless* to a crawl. Pop paused briefly before pressing the button to lower the boat into the sea. Kai watched as the brightly colored decals spelling out the name *Bad Latitude* descended toward the deep, feeling much like he was about to lose a very good friend. He spied the key in the ignition as the hull touched down and made his move.

The clip released allowing the sling to let go setting the boat adrift. At the same instant, Kai took three running steps, bounded across the transom of *Reckless* and hurtled through the air, landing on the deck of *Bad Latitude* as it began its drift. He scrambled to the helm, slammed the palm of his hand against the tilt button and lowered the two hundred fifty horsepower motor into the wash, while twisting the key in the ignition. The engine kicked over immediately as Kai turned to face *Reckless,* the distance between the two boats increasing rapidly. Jack ran to the stern screaming for Kai to return but it was no use. Kai gave a brief wave, aimed Jack's boat on an angle facing the opposite direction and plunged into the darkness.

Pop put his arm around his grandson. "We have to go full throttle or we'll get caught."

Jack, tears streaming down his face nodded and returned to the helm. He turned to look across the stern once more before pushing the CAT engines back to full speed. "There's nothing we can do," said Pop as he squeezed Jack's shoulder.

He stared dead ahead. His best friend was gone. Nothing could change that. Finally, in a choked whisper, but without looking up, he pointed to the wheel. "You'd better take over. I have to tell Val and Nan what's happened." Jack walked to the top of the stairs, pausing long enough to wipe the tears from his face. How would he break the news?

～12～
OVERBOARD

～ABANDONING BAD LATITUDE MADE *Reckless* light enough to cut through the water at top speed, easily outrunning the whirlpool and its eerie spinning lights. Dawn broke with a purple-orange glow while the seas remained calm. Pop was exhausted and called downstairs for Jack. A few minutes passed before Nan joined him at the helm. She handed him a cup of coffee, which he promptly placed in a holder without his usual cheerful thank you. Nan's eyes were rimmed red from crying. The whites of Pop's blue eyes were solid pink. He wrapped his arm around Nan and she buried her face into his shoulder sobbing softly. Finally, she stopped, dabbed at her face with a Kleenex and slowly inhaled deep breaths of salty air. Seeing the pain in her face was more than Pop could stand and he looked away trying to think of something to say.

"I loved that kid you know," said Nan.

Pop cleared his throat, his eyes leaking tears. "Yeah, me too. Let's not give up. Maybe he managed to survive somehow. How're the kids holdin' up?"

"Val is hysterical, as you can imagine. Jack's a total zombie. He won't talk at all. Rachel… well, if it weren't for her I don't know how I could have gotten through the night. She was so… so kind… so gentle and helpful. After the initial shock and tears, she helped take charge down there. What a sweetheart." Nan wiggled her hand into Pop's left arm, giving it a squeeze. "Do really you think he might have made it?"

Coconut Palms

"Dunno. Been through quite a bit of weird stuff him n' Jack. Not tryin' to give you false hope but those two have an incredible way of beatin' the odds."

Nan brightened. "Maybe you're right. We should go look for him now."

"I planned to. That's why I slowed way down. Just made sense to wait for daylight n' make sure we were outta trouble. I've tried to raise him on the radio three dozen times but haven't had any luck. I notified the Bahama Air Sea Rescue that he was missing soon after he disappeared. Where he... uh...vanished is a little out of their range so I don't know if they'll send a chopper or cutter."

"Maybe you could find him on your radar thingy," said Nan.

"That boat wouldn't show up on the screen unless we were right on top of it. Too small. Besides, the radar was knocked out last night. So was the built in GPS."

"How have you been navigating?"

"Small hand-held unit. It was off, so it wasn't damaged. It's light enough now to start searchin' so I'll bring 'er about n' get started. Don't say anything just yet. It'll take a couple hours to get anywhere near where we lost him." Pop lifted the coffee mug and took an appreciative sip. "Wow that hits the spot."

"Do you need anything else?" asked Nan.

"Yeah I could use a thirty minute power nap. If I set the course, could you run the boat for a little while? I'll crash up on the bow so I won't bother the kids."

"Set the course and speed and go get some rest. I'll take her from here, Captain."

Pop turned the boat and re-set the throttles. He drained his cup and returned it to the holder before giving Nan a kiss. "Any problem, wake me up, no matter what." He walked to the bow and stretched out on a padded equipment box. Sixty seconds later, Pop was asleep.

Jack pulled a clean T-shirt over his badly bruised chest and climbed the stairs to the deck. When he saw Nan at the helm, he limped over. "What's the matter? Where's Pop?"

Nan tried to conceal her worry. "Everything's okay. Pop needed a break. Are you alright?"

"No, I feel like crap. My best friend is probably dead, his girlfriend is downstairs still crying, my boat's gone and it's my fault."

"First of all, nothing is your fault. Get that out of your head right now. I've always said you were the second most stubborn Rackham, right behind your grandfather. I would think you'd be even more stubborn now and refuse to give up on Kai. Maybe he's out there looking for us," said Nan.

"You think he might be okay?"

"Haven't you noticed that we're sailing east or did you assume I didn't know what I was doing behind the wheel and made a wrong turn?"

"I didn't pay attention to which way we were headed. You really think he made it?"

"Yes I do and have a brilliant idea if you'd care to hear it."

"Okay. Spill it, Granny," teased Jack. The smile wasn't his best, but better than nothing.

"No, no, forget it now."

"Geez, I'm only kidding!"

"I was thinking. Kai's pretty smart …"

"Not smart enough to…uh…never mind."

Nan gave Jack the *zip your mouth* signal and continued. "He's probably heading west, looking for us, while we head east, looking for him. If we put up the sails, that would give him a better chance of spotting us on the horizon. You and Val could climb the mast and be lookouts. We should sail in a zigzag pattern to cover more area. Sound like an idea?"

Jack kissed the top of Nan's head while hugging her tight, lifting her off her feet. "How did Pop get somebody as smart as you?"

Nan laughed. "Dumb luck I guess. Thanks for the cracked ribs. We'd better get moving."

"How about if I take over here while you check on Val and Rachel. We'll have his butt back aboard *Restless* in time for lunch." Jack was grinning, the aches and pains gone.

An hour later, the masts and rigging were in place and the sails unfurled. Rachel helped Nan put things in order in the cabin while Val climbed to the top of the yardarm, a pair of binoculars dangling from a strap around her neck. She scanned the open water looking for Kai with a renewed sense of hope. Jack turned the helm over to Pop and joined her.

"Do you really think we'll find him?" asked Val.

"More than likely, he'll find us. We just have to be patient. He should know to go west, so we should cross paths. At the very least, he'll get to one of the islands."

"How's he going to find land out here? Look, there's nothing but water."

"Val, you have to chill. *Bad Latitude* has GPS, a compass and radio. There are charts stored under the helm along with flares and a survival pack. He's carrying one hundred and twenty gallons of fuel onboard and the T-top will protect him from the sun. Trust me, if he got away from the whirlpool, and I think he did, he'll manage just fine. Be positive." Jack wasn't sure if he was trying to convince Val or himself. "We need to take care of look-out duty in shifts. No longer than an hour at a time."

"I'm okay, Jack. It's not exactly comfortable, but it's not bad."

"My point is, after awhile, everything's going to look the same and you're apt to miss seeing him. We need to take turns and get some rest between shifts."

"Okay, that makes sense. I'll stay up here 'til nine and we'll switch then," said Val.

Jack climbed down the ratlines to the deck. Pop was eating breakfast standing at the helm. "Hey Pop, how long do you think it'll take to get back to where we dropped *Bad Latitude*?"

"We're makin' wide angular sweeps so it could take all day. Hopefully we'll find him, or he'll find us, before nightfall."

"Maybe we should rig something up in case he has to find us in the dark," said Jack.

"Yeah, how 'bout a bunch of party lights? We can hang 'em on the masts n' tie them down to the gunwales."

"We have party lights on board?"

"Yep. Got a bunch of 'em. See if Rachel can come up top and help me out while I drag the stuff out."

"Okay, then I gotta go on watch duty up top. Val's going to be ready for a break at nine."

Rachel joined Pop at the helm. "Jack said you needed some help?"

"I need you to keep us on course while I rig somethin' together."

"I...I don't know how to drive this thing!"

"Rachel, you wouldn't be drivin', you'd be sailin'. All you need to do is watch this compass n' steer so the needle stays on this mark," Pop explained as he pointed to the instrument panel. "I'm gonna be ten feet away so don't worry."

Val walked into the galley, looking annoyed. Nan had just finished cleaning up. "Be patient Valerie, we have a ways to go."

"I know, it's not that. My butt's killin' me and I'm so thirsty."

Nan watched Pop as he carried a large box through the salon before turning her attention back to Val. "Sit down and rest up. Drink plenty of water or Gatorade."

"Nah, I need to get back. Just need some water or something. I'm okay."

"How're you makin' out over there Rachel?" asked Pop as he set the box of lights down gently onto the deck.

"Fine, this is kinda fun."

"Good, we'll turn you into a sailor yet." Pop walked to the mast and tossed a rope up to Jack. "Tie this off to the spar and I'll hook the guide up down here."

"What's that?" asked Val as she walked onto the deck.

"A bosun's seat. It'll be more comfortable and easier to get up n' down. Alright Val, hop on n' I'll hoist you up with these pulleys. When you get to the top, wrap the rope like this," he said as he demonstrated.

"Quite the inventor," said Nan watching Val wave as she reached the top.

"I didn't make it. It came with the boat. Shoulda remembered it before."

The afternoon wore on with no sign of Kai or *Bad Latitude* as they started their second pass. Pop and Rachel took turns at the helm, while Jack, in between lookout duty stints, strung the party lights from the masts to the gunwales. The optimistic mood from the morning had given way to doubt as the sun slouched further downward. Warm breezes turned steadily cooler as the brilliant waters lost their color with the setting sun. Val felt exhausted and defeated as she collapsed into a deck chair near the helm.

"He's going to find us tonight," said Rachel. "The lights will draw him our way."

"I hope you're right. Better be. I can't stand it anymore," muttered Val. "I'm sure he's okay, like Pop said, he has a knack for survival. You're doing a great job handling the boat."

"Pop's been showing me how all these gizmos work, and some basic tricks about navigation. Says knowing this kind of stuff might come in handy some day."

Val forced a smile. "He never skips a chance to teach, or give orders. Not sure which he prefers."

Jack turned the lights on early; he didn't want to fumble in the dark looking for problems. They worked fine. He smiled thinking *Reckless Endeavor* probably looked like a floating used car lot. If Kai didn't find them tonight, chances were bleak that he ever would.

"It's almost ten o'clock, Jack. You need to get some sleep," said Pop.

"I'm okay."

"Well, I'm not. I'll need a break soon. Set your clock for one, that'll give you a few hours sack time," said Pop. "Nan's gonna stay up here n' keep me company." There was no point arguing and Jack went below to rest.

Kai was riding west staring at nothing but black water under a midnight sky crowded with bright stars. The radio had been out of commission ever since the antenna had snapped in half. The whirlpool had sucked *Bad Latitude* partway into its swirling fury. After spinning counterclockwise for nearly an hour he had worked the boat toward the edge of the whirlpool, finally escaping as if shot from a cannon. The release had almost capsized him. By now, Val and the Rackhams must have assumed he'd been lost at sea. Jumping onto *Bad Latitude*, he decided, had been a very stupid move.

A new thought burned its way into his mind. *What if they'd turned around trying to rescue me?* He knew *Reckless* wasn't nearly as maneuverable as *Bad Latitude*. If Jack had tried to chase Kai down, the odds were good that the whirlpool would have swept them away and Val, Rachel and the Rackhams could now be lying on the bottom of the Atlantic. He staggered at the mental picture before stepping to the gunwale to throw up. *How could I have been so dumb?*

Kai reached over the side into the sea, cupped his hands and splashed water on his face. After a few deep breaths, he returned to the wheel. Scanning the open water he thought he saw bright lights ten degrees northeast. He was sure that he was seeing things from the effects of exhaustion and the start of dehydration, and pulled his shirt up over his face to use as a towel before trying to focus again. The lights were still there, maybe brighter. Grabbing the binoculars, he walked to the bow and looked again. A chill went through him. *What if it's that light thing from the whirlpool? If that's what it is, there's gonna be huge waves out in front of it.* He returned to the helm and throttled back to idle, waiting to see which way the lights were moving. *What if it's the Rackhams out there lookin' for me?* Whatever it was, it seemed headed his way. *Reckless only has a few spotlights; it's got to be that whirlpool.* Kai turned on the floodlight at the back of the T-top to compare the GPS readings with the chart he'd found under the helm. He had two choices. Investigate the lights or run south toward the islands. *I'd never make it through those big waves in this boat and I'm down to a quarter tank of fuel.* The wind was strengthening and he made his decision.

Kai punched in the coordinates of the closest island, tucked the chart behind the windshield and spun the wheel hard to starboard as he shoved the throttle forward to full speed. *Bad Latitude's* bow lurched upward into the air before reaching plane, slamming with a heavy slap against the light rollers, leaving behind a frothy wake shimmering in the fading glow of the stern. *Reckless Endeavor*, lights blazing, sailed on toward Kai's abandoned position.

13
DAYBREAK'S KISS

"LOOK TO THE PORT SIDE. Do you see a light?"

Pop stepped to the gunwale and squinted through his binoculars. "Yeah, I see it. Seems like somethin's bobbin' around out there. It's probably a fisherman. "Well, now he's movin'. Whoever it is, they're in a big hurry n' they're headin' south."

"Maybe it's Kai," said Nan.

"If so, why we would he run off like that? Don't you think he'd want to check us out?"

Jack shuffled onto the deck from below. "What's going on?"

Nan explained. She wondered why Jack looked up at the sails and rigging as she spoke. "It was Kai," he said.

"Well, why'd he go n' hightail it?" asked Pop.

"Which way did he go?"

"Due south, at first anyway. Hard to tell in the dark. Only saw it for a minute. Come on, what are you drivin' at?"

"The lights must've scared him off. We're all lit up and he thought he was heading toward the whirlpool again."

"What are you talkin' about?" Pop was rubbing eyes.

"You guys were down below when the whirlpool was bearing down on us. Kai was the first to see it. Somewhere, maybe in the middle of it, were these bright swirling lights. They faded when we started pulling away. He probably saw all the lights we strung up here and thought we were the whirlpool headed his way."

Pop punched a few keys on his laptop and pulled up a chart on the screen before checking their position with the handheld GPS. "Okay, let's assume you're right and it was Kai. If we follow him south, we should be within sight of this island by morning. My guess is, again assuming it was him, he would head here," he said pointing at the screen. "Let's set our course and see what happens."

"Should we drop the sails again and use the big engines?" asked Jack.

"Nah, too much work and no benefit. We won't see anything before daybreak and there's no sense gettin' Val all worked up for nothin'. Take the wheel n' keep 'er steady, I'm gonna get some rest. See you in the morning." Pop started for the salon. "We'll send Rachel topside to give you a hand. Girl's a natural-born sailor if you ask me."

"That's okay. I'll be fine."

Nan started to say something but Pop interrupted. "You're not stayin' up here by yourself. And don't tell me you're fine."

Jack nodded and said goodnight. Rachel joined him at the helm ten minutes later. She was barefoot, wearing a Flagler College sweatshirt and a pair of jeans. Her blonde hair was blowing in her eyes and she smiled awkwardly as she approached. Jack felt a brief twinge of guilt as he stared at her. He wanted to kiss her but lowered his eyes pretending to check the GPS.

"Nan sent you some sandwiches," said Rachel as she placed a small cooler on the table next to the laptop. "She said you haven't eaten anything since yesterday."

"She's probably right. I haven't thought much about food since Kai disappeared." He sighed. "I guess you're sorry you made this trip."

"I'm sorry about Kai, not about the trip. I have a feeling we're gonna find him."

"Pop says you're a natural-born sailor."

"I don't know about being a sailor, but I love being out here...."

"Can you take the wheel? I've got to shut the lights down," said Jack as he moved toward a bank of switches at the side-wall of the cabin.

"...with you," she added when she thought Jack couldn't hear her. Her mind raced, keeping pace with her pulse. She was happy, content, confused and scared. *I can't stand this. Every time I get near him my heart pounds out of my chest! He's going to find out, then what?*

"You say something?" asked Jack as he returned to his seat next to the helm.

"Excuse me?" Rachel turned her face hoping Jack wouldn't see her scarlet cheeks.

"Oh, I thought you said something when I walked away."

"Maybe you'd better eat, you're hearing things. That's probably the first sign of starvation."

Jack laughed. "Whatever. I'm starved. Here, take one," he said handing her a sandwich.

Rachel wasn't hungry but accepted the sandwich. If nothing else, chewing would keep her from saying anything more to add to her embarrassment.

Jack leaned back in his seat and put his feet up before biting into the shrimp salad. He'd heard Rachel add the words 'with you' as he walked away. *Geez, she even smells great.*

The sun peeked over the horizon off the port side of *Reckless*. Jack was confident that they were less than an hour from the island, but made no move to check the GPS. Rachel had fallen asleep leaning against him as he sat behind the controls.

He had covered her with his own sweatshirt and tucked her tight against his chest with one arm hooked around her shoulder. His arm was numb. Her nap would have to end soon. There was work to do.

Ten minutes passed and Rachel stirred. Jack lifted his arm as she opened her eyes. "I fell asleep?" she asked.

"Yep."

Rachel bolted upright. "I'm so sorry, oh geez, your sweatshirt…" She shoved it toward Jack looking panicked. "How long was I sleeping? I was supposed to…I can't believe this. This is so…so embarrassing. You must think I'm some kind of idiot." She slid away and stood, her eyes refusing to make contact with his.

Jack twisted his arm a few times to get rid of the pins and needles.

"You had your arm around me?"

"Would you stop? You fell asleep a couple hours ago. Your head was leaning against me. It got chilly so I put my sweatshirt over you and stuck my arm behind your head so you'd be more comfortable. End of story," said Jack.

"I didn't say anything?"

"I don't know. You were snoring so loud…"

"I was not!"

Jack laughed. "Don't worry. You didn't talk or snore."

"Don't say anything to Val."

"What would I say?"

"I just don't want her to think…"

"Think what? You fell asleep. Big deal!"

"Big deal? You got your arm around me while I'm sleeping and it's …"

"It's what? Was I supposed to let you fall off the seat onto the deck or maybe let you freeze your rear end off? Lighten up."

Rachel sighed. "I just don't want anyone to get the wrong idea, including you. And I don't want Val to say anything to your girlfriend."

"Okay, I'll keep your secret, you keep mine," said Jack.

"What's your secret?"

"I have a few."

"Tell me." Rachel was now smiling and looking directly into Jack's eyes for the first time since waking up.

Jack looked around as if checking for an eavesdropper, held up his finger across his lips to make the shshsh sign before motioning her closer.

Rachel giggled and leaned over.

"Closer." He held up his hands to show that he intended to whisper in her ear. "I'll tell you three secrets."

She leaned over, still smiling, wondering what he was up to.

"I don't have a girlfriend anymore. Talia emailed me yesterday. She's staying in California and has a new guy," he whispered.

Rachel straightened. "Really?"

"Shshshsh! You want to hear the rest?" Jack motioned again and again she smiled and leaned forward. He whispered, a little louder this time. "I think you smell great."

"What?" She was laughing now.

"Shshshsh! Last one. Hurry up."

Rachel paused, not sure what secret number three could be. She leaned forward and turned her ear once more. Jack placed two fingers alongside her chin, gently turned her face toward his and kissed her lightly on the lips.

Startled, Rachel stepped back. "Why did you do that?"

"Sorry, couldn't help it."

"Me either," said Rachel as she wrapped her arms around his neck and kissed him.

Jack smiled. "Why'd you do that?"

"Sorry, couldn't help it," laughed Rachel. "Can I tell you a secret?"

"Again?"

"Different secret."

"Okay."

"I wanted to do that since…" Rachel turned toward the cabin door. Pop was walking up the steps to the deck. "I'll tell you later," she whispered as she took a step backwards.

"See anything unusual last night?" asked Pop.

"Nah, everything stayed quiet 'til morning," said Jack with a quick look toward Rachel. She smiled behind her hand before greeting Pop.

"Mornin' Rachel. Everything okay?"

"Couldn't be better Pop. I'd better run downstairs and get changed."

Pop shook his head. "What's she all bubbly about?"

Jack turned, facing the starboard beam. "Guess she's happy about finding Kai."

"Whaddya talkin' about. Didn't find 'im yet."

"Yeah, we did. That's my boat anchored over there," said Jack as he pointed toward a small island a half mile away.

"This is as close as I can get," announced Pop. "You'll have to use the inflatable dingy."

Jack set the bow anchor and waited for the stern to drift with the current. They were in fourteen feet of water, two hundred yards from shore. He grabbed a pair of fins and a snorkel from the locker and sat on the gunwale to gear up.

"What are you doin'?" asked Pop.

"I can swim that far. No need for the dingy."

"How do you know Kai's in good enough shape to swim back?"

"He's a better swimmer than me."

"Maybe, but he might be banged up or somethin'. Take the dingy and some supplies. He's probably hikin' around lookin' for water. That emergency pouch only held a couple of quarts."

"I'm going with you," said Val as she tied her hair into a ponytail.

Jack opened his mouth to argue and stopped himself. "Okay, but you have to get changed. You can't crawl through the bushes wearing a bikini."

"I'll be right back," said Val smiling as she ran toward the cabin door.

Rachel fidgeted, hoping Jack would ask her along. They pumped the zodiac full of air and lowered the rope ladder to the water. Pop tied a bow line off and helped Jack drop the little boat and its 10 horsepower engine overboard with the davit where it bobbed a few yards from the hull of *Reckless*. Nan joined them on the deck carrying a backpack.

"Where are you going?" asked Jack.

"Nowhere. I just packed some stuff for you to take ashore. There's some food and water inside," said Nan.

"Thanks. Guess I'm in too much of a rush. Rachel, are you going ashore with us?"

"If it's okay, yeah."

"Think you could get *Bad Latitude* over here before you go onto the island? I want to have a way to reach you in a hurry if there's an emergency. Here, take this along," said Pop as he handed over the spare key to Jack's boat, along with a flare gun and pair of machetes. He shrugged, "You never know."

After Jack towed *Bad Latitude* back to *Reckless*, he and the girls shoved off toward the tiny island. Rachel leaned against the side of the inflatable and dangled her arms in the crystalline waters as she watched the brightly colored sea-life below.

"You might want to keep your hands in," said Jack.

Seconds after Jack's warning, a nine-foot Caribbean Reef Shark swam under the boat; gliding within inches of Rachel's outstretched hands. She let out a scream as she pulled back from the side. "Did you see that? It was … it was a shark."

"Reef shark. They're not usually aggressive, just curious," said Jack. "Tons of 'em in these waters, you just have to be sensible."

"And you were going to swim to shore?"

"Did the shark try to bite?"

"No, I don't think so."

"See, just curious. You have to be calm and confident. When you're underwater, act like you belong. Bad things happen when you panic."

"What about Kai? Val told me he was attacked last year."

"That was different. He was bleeding when that happened; besides, that was a Bull Shark, lots more aggressive."

The dingy skidded across the sandy bottom through the surf and, after dragging it away from the water's edge, Jack hefted the backpack and walked ahead, into the trees.

"How do you know to go this way?" asked Val.

Jack paused, taking on a faraway look. "I don't know. It's weird, like there's something calling me in this direction."

"Huh?"

Jack laughed. "Footprints. I followed his tracks to this spot. It's a small island, shouldn't take long to find him. Come on, let's go get him."

"Think there are wild animals out here?" asked Rachel.

"I don't think there's enough water here for any animals. We might see some lizards, birds and snakes, probably nothing bigger than that."

"Snakes?"

"They won't bother you unless you step on one."

"Great, not worried now," said Rachel as she followed Jack and Val into the mangroves.

～14～
THE LAST RESORT

～KAI TRUDGED THROUGH THE dense foliage barefoot. There were no trails to follow; the island was deserted, nearly lifeless. He reached the top of a small hill and sat at the base of a coconut palm to pull tiny stickers from the soles of his feet. His uphill trek had started at first light, an hour after anchoring offshore. *Bad Latitude's* fuel tank was nearly empty and the emergency water pack had run out the night before. Finding fresh water was going to be tough. The painful cramps in his calves and thighs were an early sign of dehydration. *Guess I shoulda paid better attention to those survival shows on TV* he thought to himself. He leaned back and stretched his aching legs, as he stared up the trunk of the tree. *That's it! Coconuts!*

Climbing the coconut palm in bare feet and with muscle spasms was a painful ordeal, but he managed it. His skin was scraped raw as he worked his way downward, gripping tightly with his arms and legs around the rough trunk. Six coconuts lay scattered at the bottom. Finally, his feet hit the ground and he plopped down in a heap. After catching his breath, he chopped through the wood-like shell of the largest coconut with his dive knife. It was a lot of work for little reward. He reached the dark brown layer of husk and stabbed at its top until it broke through to the milky center. With his head tilted back, he held the coconut a few inches above his mouth and gulped the warm semi-sweet liquid as the milk spilled down his chin and onto his chest. Reaching for another coconut and his knife, he thought about his friends and his predicament. *Wonder if anyone's lookin' for me? Maybe I should build a fire and some kind of shelter. I should collect stuff…* his chin dropped and he dozed fitfully in the morning sun's gentle heat.

The Last Resort

"He's probably hiked to higher ground looking for water. These little islands usually don't have springs. That's why they're not inhabited," explained Jack as they climbed up the gentle incline toward a thick stand of palms.

"But he could die without water," said Val.

"He might be a little dehydrated, not enough to kill him. I'm thinking he'd head for those palms up there…"

"To get the milk from the coconuts," finished Rachel. "That's why you didn't waste any time walking around the beach."

"Exactly. He's searching for water, food, & shade. Look, he cut through this way where these scrub branches are bent and separated. We should catch up with him pretty soon."

He must be delirious. Someone was calling his name from somewhere far away. It sounded like Jack. Maybe it was Val. Maybe it was both. It was louder now. Impossible. He was alone and not a soul knew where he was. His mouth was dry again and his body ached. It was hot. The trees blocked the breeze. He was shaking. Why was he shaking?

"Kai!"

"Come on. Stop foolin' around. Here, drink this."

Kai raised his head, squinting as he opened his eyes. He could see Jack, Val, and Rachel kneeling down, surrounding him. Jack was shoving something in his face.

"Kai, it's us."

"What? How'd you guys find me?" Kai guzzled the water in breathless gulps then smiled at a tearful Val. "Were ya worried 'bout me?"

Val hugged him tightly as a waterfall of tears let loose. "I thought you were at the bottom of the ocean," she wailed.

"I was worried about you guys too. Wasn't sure if the big boat outran the whirlpool."

Jack was standing and reached his hand out to pull Kai to his feet. "What were you thinking jumping on the boat like that?"

"I don't know. It all happened so fast. I was sure *Bad Latitude* was fast enough to get clear, so I figured I'd run her hard to the west, get you on the radio and we'd meet up once we were out of trouble. Problem was, the boat spun on me before I could juice the throttle and I got caught at the edge and played merry-go-round for about an hour. When I managed to get free and reach calm water, I found out the radio antenna was snapped, so I couldn't even call out a *Mayday*."

"Okay, but you didn't answer my question. When we cut it loose, why'd you jump aboard?"

Kai sighed. "Lotsa good times on that boat. Maybe I'm bein' weird, but if it weren't for that boat, you n' me wouldn't be here today. There, now go ahead n' tell me I'm an idiot."

"So you risked your neck to save a machine. Very noble," teased Jack. "Let's get out of here, Nan and Pop have been really upset."

"They were worried about me too?"

"Uh, not exactly. Pop said he wanted to dock yesterday instead of crisscrossing these waters looking for you. He said you messed up his whole schedule. You know how he is about plans working out just right."

"He said that? But Nan was worried 'bout me though, right?"

"She was at first, and then realized she had an appointment on Grand Bahama and wanted to get underway. Val's the one that convinced them to let us search for another twenty minutes. We got lucky when we spotted *Bad Latitude* anchored on the west side of this little island."

"Geez, they weren't worried?"

"You moron, they were in a panic. Everybody was. We sailed all over the place, even hooked up a bunch of lights hoping you would see us at night."

"That was you?"

"What was me?"

"Last night I saw a bunch of lights movin' toward me. I thought it was that whirlpool thing again, or maybe the death ship from last summer, so I hauled south as fast as I could n' ended up here. Boat's just about out of gas by the way."

"So you ran away from us after all that. *Bad Latitude's* already back in the cradle, probably getting re-fueled."

"You guys swam all the way from *Reckless*?"

"No we used an inflatable dingy."

"Good thing. The water's teemin' with sharks. I hugged the bottom all the way to shore, never even surfaced for air, and they still followed and bumped me." Kai grabbed Val's hand and tugged her toward the thicket. "Better get movin' so Mr. Rackham can chew my butt. That'll be about as bad as gettin' lost at sea."

Rachel moved next to Jack as they started their walk toward the beach. "What was he talking about? A death ship?"

"Long story."

"Another creepy adventure?"

"Part of one," said Jack.

Rachel couldn't convince him to explain the story of the *death ship,* even after begging. "It must be something you guys made up then," she pouted.

"Guess you'll have to read the book and see for yourself," said Jack.

"What book?"

"The one Pop wrote about last summer's treasure hunt. It's called *BAD LATITUDE*."

"You're impossible."

"Sometimes."

The closest Kai came to a butt-chewing was a bear-hug and weary threat from Pop. "I ought to drop you off in Key West. THAT was the dumbest … ah… forget it."

Val wouldn't let go of Kai's hand. Nan smiled. "Valerie, I think Kai would have an easier time eating lunch if he could use both hands," she said.

"Should we sail to Bimini and hang out a few days or head straight for Grand Bahama?" asked Pop as everyone finished their meal.

"I thought we were going to the Bahamas," said Rachel.

"Bimini is part of the Bahamas. So was the place where we found Kai. There are about seven hundred islands, but only a couple dozen are inhabited," said Pop.

"I say we stop at Bimini. It would be cool to dive along the edge of the underwater cliff," said Kai.

Rachel looked puzzled. "Underwater cliff?"

"Yeah. There's a drop off of thousands of feet to the bottom of the ocean," said Kai.

"Sounds dangerous."

"Could be. I've seen pictures but it would be cool to see it for myself. How 'bout you, Jack?" asked Kai.

"I say let the girls decide."

"Let's stop," said Val. "I don't know about diving the cliff but I want to check out the coral and the colorful fish." She turned to face Rachel, "We can stay in the shallow water."

"I guess I'll give it a try. What you think, Nan?"

"It's unanimous. I'm anxious to take pictures of the reefs," said Nan.

"You can dive?" asked Kai.

"Think I'm too old?"

"No, but geez…" Kai's face turned bright red.

"I have a new underwater camera and love to snorkel. You guys can keep all of that diving gear."

"What about sharks?" asked Rachel.

"You'll see plenty of them," said Jack.

"I was afraid you were going to say that."

"Okay, then it's settled. Let's get underway. Should make Bimini in a couple of hours," said Pop as he stood from the table.

They anchored off the shore of Bimini for three days of snorkeling and diving. Kai and Jack ventured along the edge of the cliff while Val and Rachel explored the reefs lining the shallows. Rachel eventually learned not to panic at the sight of a shark, even those curious enough to swim close enough to touch. Nan snapped hundreds of pictures of brightly colored fish as they darted through the tropical waters. Pop snorkeled with Nan. He didn't have much use for tanks and regulators, unless he needed them to reach something of value, like lost treasure.

On the afternoon of the fourth day, they pulled anchor and set sail for the southwest corner of Grand Bahama. They arrived as dusk settled in.

"Furl the sails boys, we'll head into that deep-water lagoon over there to starboard in a few minutes," said Pop as he started the auxiliary engine. He made a quick call from his cell phone.

Ten minutes later *Reckless Endeavor* pulled alongside a floating dock where Pop spun the boat one hundred and eighty degrees, pointing the bow toward the open sea. A man and woman smiled and waved as the big schooner inched closer to the platform that bobbed under a garish blue and pink sign declaring their destination as *The Last Resort*. Jack tossed the lines in their direction and the pair tied them off at the cleats. A gangplank with railings was quickly secured over the gunwale as Pop shut down the motor. Nan was the first to hurry off to the dock and hugged the man and woman as if they were old friends. Pop was next and the greeting, again, was warm and enthusiastic. Jack had no clue as to who the two people might be, and shrugged toward Kai.

"Kids, I want you to meet our very good friends Eb and Flo," announced Pop. "This is my grandson Jack, you've heard all about him over the years. And this is Kai, and Valerie; we usually call her Val, and over here, trying to hide, is Rachel."

Kai whispered to Jack, "Eb and Flo? *The Last Resort*? Are they kiddin'?"

Pop scowled as he looked at Kai. "Eb and Flo own this resort. The marina, the island cottages, the restaurant, it's quite a nice piece of paradise. They also happen to serve the best conch fritters in the world."

Jack reached out and shook Eb's hand. The man was tiny, maybe an inch over five feet and his bald head peaked to point. Flo, on the other hand, was a foot taller than her husband and outweighed him by a hundred pounds. Her hair was dyed fluorescent orange, and clashed with, well, everything.

"It is wonderful to finally meet you Jackson," said Eb. His voice was deep and thunderous, not what Jack expected from someone so little. "I am Ebenezer Kerly."

At the name Kerly, Jack's eyes automatically shifted from the friendly face to the man's shiny bald head causing Eb to laugh out loud. "A rather unfortunate last name given my circumstances," he said as he rubbed the top of his head.

"Oh I cannot believe you are here on our island," squeaked Flo as she edged past her husband. She grabbed Jack in a bear hug and lifted him off his feet with no apparent effort. The image of a muscle-bound *Minnie Mouse* flashed through Jack's mind as the air emptied from his lungs in one giant whoosh. He heard Kai snicker in the background.

"How long have we been friends Eb?" asked Pop.

"Nearly forty years."

Pop explained to Jack, "Me n' Eb worked together back in the day. Lost touch for a number of years then bumped into each other right after you were born. Eb and Flo have been handling a little project down here for us. Guess you could say they're helpin' us to get set for retirement."

"You've been retired for years."

"Yeah, but this time, I mean really retired."

Nan interrupted. "Why don't we get settled for the night?"

"You're going to have dinner with us, I hope," said Flo.

"Absolutely. I can't think of anything I would enjoy more," said Nan.

"Eb, were you able to find someone to keep an eye on things?" asked Pop with a slight sideways nod toward *Reckless*.

"No worries, it's all taken care of, my friend."

Eb and Flo ushered the group to a cluster of three pristine cottages, all facing the sea, set in a semi-circle around a private swimming pool. Pop and Nan were led to the bigger yellow cabin, the boys to the blue one. Val and Rachel shared the pastel pink bungalow in the middle. All of the houses were comfortably furnished and decorated in keeping with the flavor of the islands. Everything was maintained to perfection.

After hauling the luggage from *Reckless* to the cabins, two men wearing fatigues and carrying rifles walked across the dock and boarded the big schooner. They took turns rotating from bow to stern keeping watch from the deck as nightfall advanced.

Shortly before midnight, a boat motored back and forth past the entrance of the lagoon at trolling speed. A man stared through a pair of night-vision binoculars at the guards stationed aboard *Reckless*. He lowered the glasses and shook his head. "Rackham's being very cautious. He must be on to something big. They've got armed guards posted onboard." The man with the thick white streak of hair let out a short cough. "This might be more difficult than I'd expected," he said to the man behind the wheel. "Let's get outta here. I've gotta rethink this."

～15～
FLYIN' HIGH

～IT SOUNDED LIKE A BATTERING ram pounding against the cabin door. Rachel looked at the clock on the nightstand and groaned. The clock's face said it was almost seven. Val stumbled across the room, opened the door a few inches and, after a brief pause, pulled it back allowing Nan to enter the cabin.

"The day is wasting away. Let's get some breakfast and head into town. It's about time you girls learned how to shop."

"It's too early," said Val with a yawn.

Rachel pulled the covers over her head. "I'm so tired. We were up late."

"The boys have been gone since daybreak."

"Where'd they go already?"

"Spear fishing."

Val rolled her eyes. "Those two are going to sprout gills."

"You might be right. I'll wait for you by the pool. Flo is taking us," said Nan as she walked out.

Rachel swung her legs over the side of the bed. "Where do these people get their energy?"

"When do we start looking for the treasure Pop?" asked Jack as he secured a spear gun inside the rack underneath *Bad Latitude's* gunwale.

"We leave port tonight, while everyone's asleep."

"Why at night?"

"There's someone payin' real close attention to what we're doin'. The guards noticed 'em. We're gonna get underway when they think we're sleepin' so they can't follow us."

"Guards?"

"Yeah. Eb hired a couple of off duty policemen to keep an eye on things for me. They said they saw two guys in a Boston Whaler pass by last night real slow. One of them was checkin' things out with a pair of binoculars. The guards acted oblivious so our would-be visitors would think I was only worried about keepin' the boat safe."

"What makes you so sure someone's watchin' us?" asked Kai.

"I've seen the same boat the guards described four times in the last five days. I think it's those two crewmembers that abandoned Captain Sutton the day he delivered *Reckless*."

Rachel and Val joined Nan at the poolside table and hurried through their breakfast. Flo arrived as they finished. "Is everyone ready?"

Val was surprised when Nan followed Flo toward the dock. "Where are you going?"

"To the dock," said Nan.

Rachel shrugged and walked along. "So we're going by boat?"

Flo laughed in her usual high-pitched squeak. "A boat would take too long child. You don't get airsick do you?"

"Airsick?"

"From flying," said Nan.

"We're going to fly?" asked Val.

"In my seaplane," said Flo pointing toward a bright yellow plane with twin propellers bobbing in the lagoon ten yards from the dock.

"You're kidding right?" asked Rachel.

"It's the best way to get around down here," answered Nan.

"And you take off and land in the ocean?"

"When it's calm, like today," said Flo.

Out of nowhere, two of the resort workers appeared and began tugging on the mooring line. Within a few minutes, the port side pontoon was bumping gently against the dock pilings.

"I don't know if I can do this," said Val.

"Oh come now, it's a beautiful way to see the islands, the changing colors of the sea and the white sandy beaches. We're also going to take a look at the latest Rackham project from the air," said Nan with a tiny nod toward Flo.

Flo smiled. "I am a very good pilot, much better than Ebenezer."

"I'll go if Rachel goes," said Val.

"Gee thanks. Make me the bad guy. Guess that settles it," said Rachel.

Val and Rachel boarded first and climbed into the back seat. Nan was next and sat up front securing her seat belt as Flo eased in behind the controls. "There are headsets under your seats. If you plug them into those jacks at the armrests, you can listen in while I tell you where we're flying. It will also help drown out the noise of the propellers."

The girls put on the headphones, and gripped the armrests until their knuckles turned white. They watched as Flo flipped through an array of switches and toggles on the plane's control panel before giving the thumbs up signal to the two men holding long aluminum poles which they then used to push the plane away from the dock. Once clear, Flo started the engines and turned the small plane to face the open sea. As the hum of the engines grew louder, the vibration inside the cabin intensified before the craft raced its way along the surface of the lagoon. With a slight shudder the seaplane lifted off gaining altitude before veering north with the starboard wing tipped downward toward the ocean.

"Better not show off yet, Flo or the girls are going to lose their breakfast," said Nan.

Flo giggled and nodded before leveling out. "Shall we fly over the Rackham *project* first?"

"I was hoping we could do that. Will it take long to get there?" asked Nan.

"Five minutes."

Nan turned in her seat to face Rachel. "Are you kids doing okay?"

Rachel looked at Val then gave a weak smile and a nod yes.

"It's coming up on your side," said Flo, her hand pointing past Nan's face. "I'll take a few slow passes & stay low so you can see it. Eb's there now. He was meeting with the marble installers. Look there he is, waving up at us."

Nan spoke into her microphone. "Girls, look down there at this little island. It's on my right side now but we'll circle around a few times so you can both get a better peek."

"What are we looking at?" asked Val.

"It's the new Rackham house. We're hoping it will be done by the end of the summer," said Nan.

"You and Pop are moving?"

"Nothing that drastic. We wanted a private little place where we could get away, something with deep water and plenty of space to keep *Reckless*. That's what I wanted anyway. Mr. Rackham said he liked the idea of owning an island but I think he was more interested in a tax shelter."

"It's huge. Is it bigger than the other house?" asked Rachel.

"There's more property but the main house is a bit smaller," answered Nan.

"So you have to go everywhere by boat. Doesn't that kinda scare you?"

"See over there? It looks like a road with a big white building alongside. That's an airstrip. We bought a small plane so we can go back and forth between St. Augustine whenever we want. Pop just got his pilot's license last winter. Oh look, the pool is almost finished."

"You guys are crazy," blurted Val.

"Maybe a little."

Rachel stared out the window. There were workers all craning their necks upward watching the plane circle. She noticed they had built a very long dock with what looked like an ornate boathouse at one end. It seemed bigger and fancier than the one in Florida. Behind the main house, with an opposite view of the water, was a smaller building still in the framing stage. "What's that?" she asked.

"That's the guest house. When people visit, they like to have their own space."

"Don't you think it's…uh…a little much? It must be costing a fortune."

"It is."

"Well, what if something happened and you …."

"Like if we ran out of money?"

"Well, what would you do if you did?"

"I guess we'd change the way we live. It's only things, Rachel. That stuff doesn't make us who we are or what we're all about."

Without warning, Flo turned southeast and pulled the plane into a steep climb making the small island disappear behind them. Val clutched at her stomach as a ticklish sensation changed to nausea. Rachel closed her eyes and held on. Twenty minutes of terror passed before Flo made a perfect landing at a marina with an area designated for seaplanes. A large skiff approached and the man at the bow pointed toward a row of planes already moored. Once the plane was within one hundred yards, the man gave the signal to cut the engines by making a slashing motion across his throat.

"They'll tow us to the mooring buoy and secure the plane, then take us to shore in the skiff," announced Flo. "It will only take a few minutes. That wasn't so bad was it?" she asked with a high-pitched cackle.

Rachel finally relaxed her grip on the armrest. Val's face was the color of key-lime pie. Both girls ignored the question.

"Does Nan know we're leavin' tonight?" asked Kai.

"Yep. She's the one that suggested it. Eb's guys are loadin' up the boat with fuel and provisions while we're out here goofin' off."

"How come you didn't tell us before?"

"So you two wouldn't bug me with a bunch of questions like you're doin' now."

"Nan and the girls are staying at Eb and Flo's?"

"That's right and we're not tellin' Val or Rachel when we're leavin' either. Don't go blabbin' to 'em when we get back."

"They already know they're not goin' with us, so what's the big deal?"

"Kai, do you see that yellow plane up there doin' those crazy dips?"

"Yeah, what about it?"

"Your girlfriend's in that plane right now. Flo's flyin' it and by now Rachel n' Val are probably ready to puke. After flyin' with Flo, they'll want to get as far away from that plane as they can."

Jack turned his attention toward the seaplane. "What's she trying to do up there?"

"She's showin' 'em what a great pilot she is. Nan doesn't mind it so much but you won't get me near that yellow plane again, not unless Eb's at the controls."

"Where are they goin'?" asked Kai.

"Freeport. They were probably buzzin' over my island," said Pop.

Jack turned his gaze from the plane and stared at Pop. "Your island?"

"Uh…guess I didn't tell you about that."

"You bought an island?"

"A small one."

"For what?"

"We wanted a little getaway."

"Can't wait to see this place," said Kai.

"It's no big deal."

"Yeah right. You guys will probably build a mansion on it."

"It's not really a mansion," replied Pop.

"You mean you're already building something?" asked Jack.

"Yep. Hope to be done in a few months. Eb's runnin' the show for us. You'll see it soon enough. I didn't want to say anything 'til it was finished, but it looks like Nan couldn't keep the secret."

"Are you sellin' the place in St. Augustine?" asked Kai.

"No. Now let's change the subject. We'll run back to *Reckless* in a few hours and make sure we're all shipshape for the trip before the Rachel and Val get back. Hopefully, between Nan and Flo, they'll be worn out and want to crash early." Pop looked up and sighed. "Guess crash wasn't a good word choice under the circumstances."

They were walking through an outdoor market in the middle of Freeport when Nan saw him. It was the man with the streak of white hair and colorless eyes. Val recognized him at the same time and started to say something. Nan cut her off. "Pretend you didn't notice him."

"He saw me stare right at him," said Val.

"What's wrong?" asked Flo.

"We're being followed. You can't see him now; he must have ducked behind something." Nan described the man and explained the story of Captain Sutton's two deckhands to Flo while her eyes continued their sweep up and down the crowded street. "Maybe it's a coincidence."

"Let's split up into pairs and see if we can find him," said Rachel.

"And do what?" asked Val.

"Tell him to leave us alone."

"That'll work. Why didn't I think of that," laughed Val.

"I'll go with Flo, you stay with Nan," said Rachel.

Val repeated her question. "What do we do if we find him?"

"We'll threaten to make him ride in a seaplane with Flo," said Rachel.

"Val, let's walk up there toward that market. Rachel, you and Flo wait here and see if that creep follows. When we get to the alleyway, we'll see if there's a place to hide." said Nan.

Flo put her hand on Nan's shoulder. "Go to the street past the alley, my brothers Moe and Joe own a fish store near the corner and they can help you hide while I take care of the bad man."

Val grinned. "Moe and Joe?"

"Yes. We are triplets."

"Should I even ask about the last name?"

"GoPee."

"You're serious."

Flo laughed. "I'm serious. Don't think we weren't teased as children, though it isn't an uncommon name around the islands. We'd better get moving if we're to draw the man out."

Nan and Val approached the GoPee fish market and, fighting the urge to look behind, ducked into a courtyard. The man with the shock of white hair emerged from a nearby shop and walked briskly toward the fish store.

"Catch up to him, Rachel and distract him just before he enters the market," said Flo.

"Where are you going?"

"I'm taking a shortcut. I'll meet him near the entrance. Don't worry."

Flo raced off to the alleyway and disappeared. Rachel ran to the corner of the market, arriving in time to catch the man looking in both directions before entering. There was no sign of Flo or Nan. She walked toward the stalker determined to draw his attention. The man paused, checking to see if Rachel was alone. Satisfied, he turned slowly and stepped out to block her path. He was within ten feet when Rachel stopped and the man smiled.

"Are you lost young lady? Need some help?" he asked.

Rachel spied Flo creeping up behind. "I'm fine, just going into the fish market. Do you want tuna or dolphin?"

"What?"

"Tuna or dolphin, pick one." Rachel smiled past the man toward Flo who was in the middle of a baseball swing aiming a forty-pound tuna at the man's head. He caught her eye and turned in time to get a face full of smelly fish. He was out cold before he hit the ground.

"We make a good team," said a beaming Flo. She turned toward two men that scurried to her side. "These are my brothers Moe and Joe. They're going see that this man gets to enjoy his nap. He's going to sleep with the fishes."

Rachel's eyes widened. "You mean they're going to kill him?"

Flo laughed. "No they would do nothing like that. Your stalker will wake in a slimy bin of fresh guts and fish heads. He will smell very bad for several days." She nodded to her brothers and they carried the stalker into the market. A minute later Rachel heard what sounded like a loud wet slap followed by the slam of a wooden door. Nan and Val joined them a moment later.

"Shall we get busy ladies?" asked Nan with the hint of a smirk. "Thank you, Flo. I had no idea you batted left handed."

The girls fell into step behind Nan and Flo as they walked into the shopping district. Rachel gently elbowed Val. "Don't these people ever get rattled?"

"Uhm, no. Don't think so," answered Val.

~16~
PIRATES

~AS POP PREDICTED, Rachel and Val fell asleep early following their shopping spree. Nan didn't want to spoil Pop's sendoff by telling him about the man with the shock of white hair. Flo told Eb about the encounter and he added a second security team to the compound's patrol and gave firm instructions that they were to stay out of sight as much as possible. *Reckless* put out to sea just past midnight. A mile offshore, the sails were unfurled and the search for the Rackham treasure was underway.

"How long 'til we get there?" asked Kai.

"A few days," answered Pop absently.

"Why so long? According to the charts, it's only forty miles," said Jack.

"We're gonna play some possum. I want to make sure we're not followed, so we're stoppin' along the way to make some dives, do some fishin' and look like regular tourists."

"Aren't you taking this a little too far?"

"Nope. Did you notice Eb doubled the security before we left?"

"No."

"Well, he did. Somethin' happened and he's takin' extra

precautions all quiet-like. Wouldn't surprise me a bit if Nan knew somethin' was up. Sneaky those two."

"If there was somethin' wrong, why wouldn't they tell you?" asked Kai.

"Because they know I'd postpone the trip, maybe even cancel it," said Pop.

"Then why'd we leave?"

"I figure it this way, if the people that have been checkin' us out see *Reckless* is gone, they'll scour around tryin' to find us. Eb's got plenty of help ashore so nothin' to worry about there. Now if somebody is lookin' for us, they'll find us within a day or two. If nothin' happens within the first coupla days, I think we'll be in the clear."

"You're really serious about this," said Jack.

"Yep. And that's why I want at least one of us on deck at all times playin' lookout."

Mid-morning on the following day, they anchored five hundred yards from a small island. Jack and Kai went diving, exploring a blue hole tucked behind a coral reef, while Pop remained aboard *Reckless*. He laid the binoculars on the helm and repositioned the headset's microphone. "Jack, a boat's been shadowin' us all mornin' and now it's headin' our way. Stay below, 'til I give you the all clear."

"Be there in a minute," was the reply through the static.

"Stay underwater. That's an order."

"If there's trouble, you're gonna need help."

"What part of **stay below** don't you understand? Nothin's gonna happen. They're probably just nosin' around. I can handle this. Do what you're told."

Pop moved toward the gunwale and folded his arms across his chest waiting as the Boston Whaler approached. Below, Jack turned to face Kai and covered his mouth, giving the *don't talk* sign then tapped the side of his head to show he was thinking. After a brief pause, he pointed his index finger toward the surface and shrugged his shoulders, asking Kai what he thought they should do. Kai didn't hesitate, and stabbed his thumb upward several times. They dropped the dive bags and weight belts on the sand next to the coral and kicked up toward the hull of *Reckless*.

Thirty feet shy of the boat's bottom, Kai grabbed Jack's arm and pointed to the anchors, then to one another. Jack understood, and nodded his head. They would split up and pull the anchors in case they needed to get *Reckless* underway quickly. They could see the propeller wash of a small boat approaching overhead two hundred yards from the starboard side of the schooner. Jack swam toward the bow anchor while Kai jackknifed toward the stern.

Pop's shotgun was propped against the gunwale in plain view of the intruders. He didn't want to appear too threatening, but it wouldn't hurt to look prepared. As the Whaler pulled alongside, he second-guessed that decision. The men were the deckhands that abandoned Captain Sutton the day after *Reckless* had arrived in St. Augustine. The one with the colorless eyes and the white-streaked hair offered a crooked smile as he shut down the engine, the other picked up a coiled rope from the deck. Trouble had arrived.

"You guys lost or somethin'?" asked Pop.

"No. Just a friendly visit. Mind grabbin' the end of this rope?"

"Yeah, I do mind. I'm not too big on lettin' strangers board my boat, 'specially out in the middle of nowhere."

"Strangers? You remember us. We were the deckhands for Captain Ron, same guys that delivered your fine boat."

"Yeah, I remember. Same ones that disappeared in the middle of the night. Another reason you're not gettin' on-board," bellowed Pop. He picked up the shotgun and held it across his left forearm when he noticed the coiled rope had a galvanized steel grapple hook attached to its end.

"Where's your crew Mr. Rackham? This is too much boat for one man to sail."

"Don't you be worryin' about my crew. Now shove off before things turn ugly."

"Ah, come on, we're old friends."

"I'm not gonna warn you again, Dawson."

"So you know my name. That's not good, not good at all."

Dawson reached down and retrieved an ominous looking weapon, and aimed it at the center of Pop's chest before Pop could react. At the same time, his partner tossed the grapple across the gap between the boats. It landed behind the forward gunwale and bit into the polished teakwood with one pull.

"What do you losers want anyway?"

"We were wondering what you were searching for. Thought maybe you'd like to share. I know you're a treasure hunter. Unfortunately, for you, we don't have time to wait around so here's the deal, we take your boat, your maps, and your computers and give you a chance to swim home with maybe just a few bullet holes. Sound fair enough?"

"You're bluffin', moron."

Dawson's face darkened. "I'm the one pointing the gun. How's that make me the moron?"

"I'm not tellin' you anything. Not a chance. Whatever's below will **stay below.**"

Pop had left the headset in the on position to monitor the boys below with the lip-mic turned downward, so his part of the conversation was still transmitting loud and clear to Jack and Kai. Hearing Pop signal **stay below** was not what Jack wanted to hear. He couldn't communicate with Kai without letting Pop know that orders were about to be ignored. Turning toward Kai, he was surprised to see Kai had cut the anchor line and was now swimming toward the Whaler.

Jack swam past the bow of *Reckless*, careful to stay out of sight. He clutched the schooner's bowline with his left hand and sawed through the heavy rope with his dive knife.

Reckless was adrift as Jack reached the port side rope ladder. Trying to move noiselessly, he removed the tank and respirator, ripped off his fins, and tied them to a dangling rope to keep them from floating off and giving away his position. Before starting his climb, Jack ducked his head underwater to check on Kai who was kicking frantically toward the surface while pointing from his watch to the boat, signaling for Jack to hurry. With a quick nod to his friend, he abandoned the mask and headset and clambered up the rope ladder, carrying his six-inch dive knife in his right hand.

Jack slid over the side and tucked in behind the helm.

Pop had run out of ways to stall.

The man named Dawson continued. "Sorry it's gotta be like this, old man," he said as he switched off the safety and applied pressure to the trigger.

"Put that gun away n' we'll see who's an old man," shouted Pop as the sound of automatic fire erupted.

Jack dove from behind the safety of the helm a moment too late. He reached the starboard side in time to see Pop knocked off his feet and slammed against the base of the davit. The shotgun clattered to the deck, a few feet away. Jack, overcome with rage, grabbed the shotgun.

"Put that down, Jack. Yer grandfather'll survive lad. 'Twas a bump to his head 'tis all. Cut loose the grapple n' get us underway. We've fair winds an' followin' seas." said the stranger standing on the top edge of the boat's gunwale.

Jack stared in disbelief. The man wore multi-colored striped trousers that disappeared into the tops of a pair of high black boots. A bloodstained ruffled shirt, torn at the elbow, and a red kerchief tied around his neck completed the outfit while a polished cutlass gleamed in the sunlight as it hung from a loose fitting scabbard overlapping a twisted red waistband.

The intruder turned to face Dawson and the other man. They seemed as dumbfounded as Jack, but it didn't deter Dawson from reloading. The stranger removed a pair of ancient-looking flintlock pistols from his waistband and, with great flair, crossed his wrists, and took careful aim. Kai cut the grappling line loose as Jack started the engines.

"Here our ways divide ye bilge-suckin' vermin. Sadly, the currents will not be in yer favor. Hope ye have plenty of water stowed."

As Dawson raised the gun, it exploded from his hands. The odd-looking man aboard the Rackham's schooner stood smiling as smoke poured from his flintlocks. "Enjoy yer slow dry drift mateys," he laughed as *Reckless* motored forward. "An' be sure ye be keepin' yer bloody hands away from the water. Blood'll draw all manner of hungry sharks n' sea beasts. Aye, 'twas a fine pleasure meetin' ye."

Jack shook as he knelt next to Pop. There was no trace of blood, no sign of any wounds. How was it possible? "Who are you?" he asked as he looked up at the intruder. Pop stirred at the sound of Jack's voice.

"Shall we help this good man below decks before I be explainin' me appearance? It would be me preference to tell me story but once."

Kai stood slack-jawed at the helm. "Another freakin' ghost."

Jack helped Pop to his feet, and led him to the cabin below. "Kai, set a course twenty degrees west and flip the bow camera on. We can keep watch from the monitors downstairs." He turned to face the oddly dressed visitor. "Mister, you'd better explain yourself really fast."

Pop regained his senses. His head throbbed as he lowered himself onto the closest cushioned seat in the salon. "Jack, grab me an ice pack." He looked toward the man in the strange clothes as he placed the cold ice against the back of his head. "Okay. Who are you? How did you get on my boat and what do you want?"

Kai sat down in front of the monitor while Jack remained standing.

"Such gratitude. Ye realize sir that I, yer humble servant, shielded ye from certain death at the hands of those shiftless rogues."

Kai couldn't keep quiet. "He's another ghost I'm tellin' ya!"

"Don't be ridiculous," barked Pop. "Ain't no such thing. Put a lid on it, Kai."

"I think you were on that other boat and climbed aboard ours to steal it for yourself, leaving your partners adrift. You've heard the expression, *dead men tell no tales*?" asked

Jack as he shortened the distance between himself and the stranger.

"Jack, sit down. There were only two men on that boat," said Pop. "I watched their approach."

"Avast, indeed there were but two. May I now introduce meself without further interruption?"

"Spit it out," said Jack.

"I shall get to that in due time, young Jack…."

"How do you know my name anyway?"

"Ah, seems I've given ye too much credit for cleverness. They call me Jack, known in particular circles as Captain Calico Jack Rackham. As ye surely already know, we are related…by blood."

"It's worse than I thought," blurted Kai. "A dead relative."

"Kai, I said button it. Mr. uh, Rackham…"

"Please, call me Captain."

"Captain. Geez, listen to me. I must be nuts," said Pop.

"Kindly explain that expression… Nuts."

"Nuts! Crazy! I'm sittin' here talkin' to a complete stranger, aboard my boat, who claims he's a pirate that's been dead for almost three hundred years. That's nuts!" Pop tried to stand but winced and leaned back into his seat. "So we're both whackos, you n' me. Now explain how you got onboard and why."

"Hmmmm…nuts, crazy, whacko, I deduce that to mean insane. May I assure ye that we are neither? I am truly Calico Jack and have watched ye and yer family for many years trying to determine yer worthiness…"

"Worthiness? What does *that* mean?" asked Jack.

"So sorry. Over the years the language has changed, hence the difficulty. Worthiness means…"

"I know what the word means."

"Then please let me enlighten ye as to me purpose. First, I must remove this lead, it's quite uncomfortable." Captain Rackham cupped his hands to his mouth and coughed three times. "Pardon me bad manners gentlemen, but it seems ye require some proof of me identity. These be the projectiles that I meself absorbed in Mr. Rackham's place." He turned toward Pop displaying a handful of deformed slugs. "I apologize sir for causin' yer injury; it was truly a miscalculation. In my zeal to protect ye, I mistakenly entered part of the space already occupied by yerself, thereby causing our collision and yer most unfortunate luck."

"Please sit, Captain and walk us through this wild tale from the top," said Pop. "Jack, could you get me a bottle of water and some Excedrin please? Cap'n, would you like something to drink?"

"Ah, Mr. Rackham, devil a doubt would I give a ransom to slake me thirst with a wee dram o' rum. 'Tis one of the many curses what accompanies me through eternity."

"Oh geez, this is sick," muttered Kai as his head turned from the visitor to the monitor.

Jack handed the bottle to Pop and sat next to Kai. "Speaking of water…Captain, why did you say to those two thugs that you hoped they had plenty of water for their slow dry drift? They'll just go back to wherever they came from."

"It'd be better if ye were to ask yer friend. Mr. Kai, yer brave act is truly commendable. Ye would've made an outstanding pirate."

Jack looked toward Kai. "What's he talking about?"

"Uh, I pulled the shear pin outta their propeller so they couldn't chase us."

"Nothin' to worry about. They'll probably get towed in by a sport fisherman. These waters are usually pretty busy," said Pop.

"Hope they have a radio on board," said Kai.

"I'm sure they do."

"What is this radio?" asked the Captain.

"Wow. You're really playin' the part," laughed Pop. "Humor the Captain here and show him the radio Kai. See if you can explain how it works while you're at it."

Kai pulled the radio microphone off the unit. "You press this button and talk. Anyone within miles can hear whatever you say, as long as they're on the same channel." He turned the volume up and the sound of boaters communicating with one another crackled from the speaker.

"Outstanding, as is this vessel. I can't wait to learn more."

"Uh, one more thing, Pop," said Kai.

"What's that?"

"I unscrewed the brass plug at the stern of their boat. They're probably sinkin'."

"Reverse course! We're gonna have to tow them in."

"You're kidding! They tried to kill you Pop!"

"Mr. Rackham, I concur with young Jack. Such villains can be given no quarter on the high seas."

"Captain, I am the Captain of *Reckless Endeavor* and I give the orders around here. I'm not gonna be responsible for two men dyin' at sea. Couldn't live with myself," answered Pop. "Jack, get on the horn and put out a warning to boaters that these guys are bad news. We shoulda done that ten minutes ago. Let the Bahamas Air Sea Rescue know about 'em and give them our last position. Tell 'em they'd be drifting southe…."

"Wait. Sounds like they got picked up," reported Kai. "I just heard BASR on the radio. They're trying to keep the boat from sinking."

"Okay, let's stay on course then. We'll run under power for now and switch to sails later. Captain, would you please resume?"

"Aye, now where to begin."

"How about proving you're really a pirate," said Jack.

"Very well." The man claiming to be Calico Jack removed his shirt. "First notice me stomach and chest are riddled with some eleven holes from yer previous visitors." He turned around revealing long deep wounds running the length of his back. "And these be from the floggins at Port Royal in the days lead'n up to me hangin'." Finally he removed the kerchief from his neck. "And this, m'lad is what a man's neck looks like after his dance from the end of a rope. One more thing," he said as he cupped his hand over his eye. "Me hangin' also caused this bit o' inconvenience." The Captain removed his hand, allowing his eyeball to dangle against his cheek next to his nose. "It's quite a brutal way to die, truth be told."

Pop took a deep breath. "I'll be in the loony bin after this trip. Let's assume, for the sake of group derangement, that you survived a shooting, beating and hanging. What makes you Calico Jack Rackham?"

"Forgive me if I gave ye the wrong impression. 'Fraid I did not survive the hangin'. In fact, me death in November of 1720 is well documented."

Jack spoke up. "We already know that our ancestor, Calico Jack Rackham, died in 1720. You show up on our boat out of nowhere making some wild claim and, because you have scars on your body and know a little history, we're supposed to believe you? It's all too insane. For all I know, this whole thing was staged and you've had some make-up artist from a horror movie create your costume to make it convincing."

"Never thought of the make-up possibility, good pick up, Jack. The dude almost had me convinced," said Kai.

The Captain was confused. "Obviously I know nothing of what ye call make-up. If ye prefer I depart, so order it and I'll be takin' me leave. Me reputation as a thief and liar complicates things, so I will share with ye two things known to no man outside of this circle just to be provin' me point. Young Jack and young Kai, ye were attacked by me ship *The William* nearly one year ago in the harbor of Augustine in the waters of the Matanzas in the hours past midnight. Would ye dispute that?"

Kai's eyebrows arched, nearly disappearing into his thick mop of curly hair.

The Captain didn't wait for confirmation. "Mr. Rackham, nine summers have passed since ye yerself purchased three copper plates from a wee shop in the Carolina Territory. In fact, ye have them aboard intendin' to use them to locate the very treasure hidden away by Anne Bonny and meself prior to me unfortunate demise. Could ye deny that?"

"Make-up huh? This guy's the real deal, you dimwit," said Kai looking squarely at Jack.

"You n' your big mouth is what this is about. I'll bet you blabbed about that stuff at school and this guy's trying to cash in," said Jack.

Pop stared hard at the man. No one spoke for several seconds. The Captain broke the silence. "Gentlemen, as promised I'll be takin' me leave and wish ye all fair seas."

"We're in the middle of the ocean. Where d'ya think you're goin?" asked Kai.

"Captain Rackham, this is the strangest meeting of my life. Welcome aboard," said Pop.

"I can't believe this. Pop, the guy thinks he's a dead pirate. So what if he knows some weird secrets. This guy's a nut job," said Jack.

"Do me a favor, Kai. Take a long look at Captain Rackham and tell me what you see," said Pop, ignoring his grandson.

Kai climbed from his seat and, keeping a safe distance, stared at the Captain. Twenty seconds passed before the blood drained from Kai's face and he turned toward Pop. "It's unbelievable. I see Jack. It's his twin...only older."

～17～
CALICO JACK RACKHAM

⌒ YOU GUYS ARE ACTUALLY BUYING THIS CRAP?

"Jack, sit down and relax. Kai, turn the other cameras on, we're gonna continue our chat with Captain Rackham down here. Keep her steady at three knots," said Pop.

With an unusual display of disgust, Jack found a seat, crossing his arms defiantly across his chest. His biceps and forearms bulged to nearly twice their normal size as he clenched his fists out of view. He hoped the intruder would make one provocative move.

"Captain Rackham, please get comfortable. I'd like to hear your story, especially the part about why you're here," said Pop as he waved an open hand toward a leather chair to his right.

Calico Jack groaned slightly as he lowered himself into the chair. "Yer most kind. What is it ye'd be wantin' to know?"

Jack uncrossed his arms and edged forward. "Why not start by telling us who you really are and what you want."

The old pirate sighed. "I've covered that so far as I am concerned, m'lad."

"You mean your deciding on our *worthiness*," said Jack sarcastically.

"Yes. Truly I have watched me descendants for several generations…"

"But you're dead. Right?" interrupted Kai, still wide eyed.

"Bless me guts, ye are correct lad."

"Then how come you're not wherever you're supposed to be?"

"That, Kai, I daresn't divulge. Forbidden am I to mention anything of me time or whereabouts since me death. Suffice to say I am here to aid in yer mission."

"You say that you're here to help us, but a year ago you attempted, as you admitted, to blow Jack and Kai out of the water with cannon fire," said Pop.

"Good point," chimed Kai. "Let's see him explain that one."

"Be assured, 'twas part of a test. Mr. Rackham, ye acquired the copper plates, but made no attempt to discover their secret until yer grandson came of age. His rather incredible success one summer ago, with young Kai's able assistance, was truly impressive. Aye, me cannon, as well as me ship, were nothing more than phantoms, used for me own purposes to determine the worthiness of me involvement in this current quest. I was most taken with Jack's remarkable instincts, as well as the skilled mastery of his vessel under duress."

"You're talking gibberish. Those cannon balls barely missed us, almost flipped the boat. We were almost killed that night for the sake of a test. Doesn't make sense," said Jack.

"Jack, ye made all the right decisions, includin' aimin' yer vessel and runnin' at me ship. 'Twas a wondrous display of seamanship."

"Great. That'll go to his head," mumbled Kai.

Calico Jack paused. "I have shown ye all evidence of me hangin', told ye things known only amongst those of us gathered here this day, and appeared on the deck of this fine schooner in time to save Mr. Rackham, with no visible means of transport. There is, indeed a fabulous treasure, the whereabouts described within the puzzle of the three copper plates. It was me intent to assist in the recovery of this rare fortune having concluded that ye gentlemen are certainly able to confront the many challenges what lie ahead. Yer determination to dispute me word however, has grown quite tiresome."

"Captain Rackham, were you ever visited by a dead ancestor during your lifetime?" asked Pop.

"No sir. I see the point ye be makin' and indeed, it has merit."

"Then you can understand and excuse our cynicism."

"S'long as ye understand me time is limited and cannot be wasted with never-ending demonstrations of evidence," replied Calico Jack.

Pop stood and excused himself. He returned a few minutes later with a roll of nautical maps and the three copper discs. "Captain, these are the charts that we're using, along with these," said Pop as he handed over the three plates.

Jack jumped from his seat to stop the hand off, but Pop stopped him with his outstretched forearm. "What are you doing, Pop? You've got to be dazed from cracking your head. This is a hoax. You're not thinking straight."

"I'm not dazed, crazy, foolish or senile. This is Calico Jack Rackham, I'm sure of it, and we're gonna accept his kind offer of assistance. You're gonna pay attention n' cooperate. That goes for you too, Kai."

Kai was indignant. "I knew the guy was the real enchilada half an hour ago!"

Jack muttered to himself and shook his head. "Okay, we'll play along, but, Captain Rackham, when you turn out to be the fraud that I know you are, I'll throw you overboard myself."

"Might I suggest, with all respect of course, that ye try disposin' of me now? What purpose could a delay serve?"

Jack's face twisted in anger at the flippant challenge as he sprang toward the man seated in the chair. Calico Jack smiled, but never budged. A moment later, Jack found himself choking for breath, dragged slowly through the azure sea behind *Reckless*. Two dorsal fins followed, only yards behind his outstretched legs.

In the salon, Pop and Kai watched in horror as Jack disappeared with a loud *crack*. "Where'd he go?" yelled Kai.

Pop jumped at the dead pirate but, despite the sensation of moving forward, was unable to get within striking distance. An instant later Jack reappeared in the salon with his hands clasped together above his head as if holding a rope and his head turned looking over his shoulder. He was dripping seawater all over the carpet as he stood awkwardly next to Pop. Calico Jack waved his hand, allowing the pair to move once again and Jack and the carpet were suddenly bone dry.

Jack smiled as he lowered his arms. "Okay, you've proved your point, but I could've done without the sharks. What if I'd let go?"

"I felt that rather a nice touch," said Calico Jack. "Ye were never in any real danger."

"Whaddya talkin' 'bout? Sharks?" Kai turned toward the pirate who was now standing. "What'd you do to him?" He frowned at Jack. "Where'd you go? How come you were soaked n' now you're dry? What's goin' on?"

"I'd like to know all that myself," barked Pop not so pleasantly.

Jack took a deep breath. "One second I was reaching to grab Calico Jack; next second I was in the water behind the boat with two sharks on my tail."

Pop glared at the pirate. "Care to explain?"

"Shall we say, that I possess certain…. abilities in me current state. Young Jack rejected me previous explanations and demonstrations and decided I was a threat. It was, therefore, necessary, to modify his…. thinking. To accomplish this task, I simply controlled your minds, for only a brief moment."

"Mind control?" Kai grinned. "Can you teach me to do it?"

"Not funny, Kai! Captain Rackham, what are you playin' at here? Mind control! You think we're gonna swallow that too?" Pop's face was red, bordering on purple and his temples pulsed painfully as he glared at the old buccaneer.

Calico Jack offered a dismissive wave. "Yer grandson was not *actually* dragged before a pair of sharks. I made him imagine it, while makin' ye gentlemen *think* he had disappeared from this very room."

"You're tellin' me it was all in our heads."

"That would be accurate, sir."

"Unbelievable."

"Have I at last put the question of me identity to rest so that we may proceed with the comparison of the charts and discs?"

Everyone nodded in unison as Calico Jack moved to the table.

"I think your…what would he be…your great great great great uncle? Whatever. He's pretty cool. Think he'd teach me how to do some of that mind stuff?" whispered Kai.

"Don't know. Not much up there to work with?" said Jack, nodding toward Kai's head.

"Very funny, moron."

Pop placed the disc marked with a three on the lower corner of the map, aligning the markings with corresponding latitude and longitude designations. Once in place, he did the same with the remaining discs. Using a straight edge, he connected the lines from one etched arrow to another so that they intersected, forming a triangle. Four islands were contained within the triangle. He turned toward Calico Jack. "Am I on the right track so far?"

"Very impressive. Do ye know the next step?"

"Think so."

Moving the discs again, he positioned the arrows on the points of the triangle and made new lines with the marker and straight edge. The triangle was now divided into six portions and Pop pointed to the intersection of the three lines. "The treasure is on the southeast corner of this tiny island," he stated matter-of-factly.

Captain Rackham forced a smile and nodded slowly. "Most disappointing."

Pop winced. "Am I off by a lot?"

"Unfortunately...no."

"Well then, what's the problem?"

"Sorry, old boy. Ye have done a most splendid job of it. Magnificent in fact. I daresay I'd thought meself to have been a trifle more clever than this. Imagine leavin' behind a clue so easily solved. It's all quite awkward really."

"What makes you think it was easy? I've spent years workin' on this. It about drove me nuts," said Pop.

"I so like that new word *nuts*, makes me want to laugh when I hear it. There were two madmen in me crew on me next-to-last voyage. I s'pose ye may have called them nuts. They fought one another constantly over the rats. Had a real taste for 'em they did."

Kai's face contorted, resembling a pug. "They ate rats?"

"Of course. We all ate them when rations were low, but as normal gentlemen would; we at least killed and cleaned them first. The men I speak of preferred to eat them alive, head first no less, chewing as the rodent's feet clawed uselessly against the bloody scalawag's chin. No threat or punishment could make them abandon this roguish behavior. Both seemed oddly immune to the bites and scratches they themselves received from the filthy little devils. Alas, pressure from the crew was too much, leaving me no choice but to put them off."

"Didja make 'em walk the plank?" asked Kai.

"Walk the plank?"

"Yeah. You know, didja set up a board and make 'em walk blindfolded out over the water 'til they fell off into the ocean?"

"Why do such a thing as that?"

"I don't know! You're the pirate! Isn't that what pirates do, I mean did, when they wanted guys off the boat?"

Calico Jack laughed. "Oh lad, that would have been a sight. So sorry to disappoint, but we never went to such troubles to rid our vessel of undesirables. No, I am afraid that the way ye describe would've required much too much effort indeed."

Kai looked annoyed. "So what'd you do then to get rid of *undesirables*?"

"Uh…well, we simply…tossed them overboard."

"So that was it? Splash n' gone."

"Ah, 'twasn't always so dull. Many times, we found it a most enjoyable sport when the sharks were plentiful and seas were calm."

"Did you feed the rat eaters to the sharks?"

"No, and me sniveling crew was most disappointed. Since those disgusting fools never committed a crime against the ship or their mates, pirate law required they be given a chance to survive. I ordered them marooned, with a supply of rations and water, to an uninhabited island, free to collect and devour whatever vermin they could scrounge."

"Why didn't you just use *mind control* on them to make them stop?" asked Jack.

"Unfortunately, that talent was…not available to me in those days."

"What do you mean?"

"Now if I could 'ave controlled the thinkin' of others, would I have not used that ability to avoid havin' me neck stretched?"

Jack's curiosity was in overdrive. "So this *ability* is something you picked up from…wherever it is you can't mention?"

The old pirate smiled. "Aye, pryin' now are we, young Jack?"

"Yeah I know; you can't tell us."

"Oh but I intend to, once ye reclaim the Rackham treasure."

~18~
THE RAT EATERS

⌐THERE SHE BE, BOYS, FISHTAIL CAY. Hard to starboard n' mind the reef."

Pop scowled at the old pirate from the helm. "I've got things under control here, Captain Rackham, so button your lip."

Kai laughed out loud, as he watched the two exchange glares.

A few minutes passed before Pop gave the order to furl the sails. He engaged the engine and throttled ahead at no wake speed. "I'm bringing her about to put the stern in line with that cluster of trees. Anchor up when we're pointed due west and throw an extra at the bow. We're in fifteen feet of water and all's clear below."

"I think it possible to get closer. 'Tis a long row ahead and longer still on the return when burdened with such riches as we shall be retrieving."

Jack set the bow anchor and waited for Pop to remind Calico Jack to butt out. Instead, Pop shut down the engine and smiled at the rugged sailor. "Lower your boat Jack, and tie it off mid-ship on the port side. It's time to show our guest how we do things in this century."

Kai worked the davit controls, swinging and lowering Bad Latitude from the stern. The winch hummed as the gleaming boat touched down into the calm green-blue water. Jack revved the engine, putting some distance between the two boats before pulling alongside to catch the dangling spring line. A rope ladder hung from the side of Reckless, slapping against the hull. Kai climbed from the sailboat to join Jack on the deck of Bad Latitude, with Calico Jack a step behind.

Pop stood at the gunwale and loosened the spring line.

"Aren't you comin' with us?" asked Kai.

"Not this trip. One of us has to stay behind to keep an eye out. Keep those handheld radios turned to channel five and stay in touch. Check in with me every ten minutes or so and let me know what's goin' on." Pop tossed the line to Kai waiting below and the trio shoved off.

Jack motioned toward Kai with his chin and shot a look toward Calico Jack. Kai nodded with a grin and grabbed onto the bow rail as Jack pushed the throttle forward as far as it would go. The boat's bow shot upward out of the water and they jetted toward the tiny island, reaching plane in a couple of seconds. The pirate never lost his balance or footing and stood at the stern as if nothing had happened.

"Would ye be thinkin' it sport to lose me overboard?"

"Uh, well, we're just joking around."

Bad Latitude approached the shallows and Jack slowed to a drift before hitting a switch to raise the outboard engine, barely keeping the propeller submerged. "Anchor up Kai, we'll let the current swing the stern toward shore." When the anchor was set, Jack cut the engine and reached for a coil of rope on the rear deck. As he gripped the line, a black boot stomped down on his hand and Jack dropped to a knee.

The pirate stared down at him with a wicked sneer. "No more jokes, as ye call them. Yer mind holds no secrets from me."

Jack stood, ignoring the pain in his hand. Kai joined him, ready to help. "What's in this for you, Captain?"

"Whatever do ye mean, lad?"

"You've been dead for three centuries. What's hidden away on this island that you need so badly?"

"The Rackham fortune must be recovered by a Rackham. Death cheated me the opportunity to raise me son. His mother, unfortunately, saw fit to keep the secret of the treasure from him, despite me complaints."

"How could you complain if you were dead?" asked Kai.

"I visited her dreams."

"You mean her nightmares."

"Those as well."

"You haven't answered my question," said Jack. "What's in it for you to see us collect your treasure?"

"When the gold is recovered these things will be made known."

"Not an answer. Kai, let's head back to Reckless. The Captain can stay here."

Calico Jack sighed. "There is a particular piece hidden away, a mere trinket, that is of great importance to me. Ye have me solemn oath that the treasure shall be yours, except for that single object."

"What will that do for you?"

"It will be used to pay a debt and release me from me bonds."

"This is too weird," said Kai. "We don't need this, let's go."

"Have I not explained that details of me days since me hangin' cannot be revealed? When the gold is recovered, me penance will be complete, bringing me great relief. I can speak of this no further."

Jack rubbed the back of his hand. "I don't trust you."

"Aye, ye be not the first to utter such words, an' deservedly so. A scalawag am I and forever shall be but this task is me last chance to…make amends. Leastways let me show ye the wealth that waits."

"Lead the way," said Jack as he grabbed a nylon bag and climbed over the gunwale into the surf.

"Jack, this is stupid. We're already rich," said Kai. "Let's pull the plug on this insanity and go back."

"It's not about the treasure. Now I need to know why this is so important and why we're really here."

The pirate's features softened. "Curiosity. A natural Rackham trait. Follow me mates."

Pop paced with a cigar clamped between his teeth and a pair of binoculars around his neck. Thirty minutes had passed with no radio communication. He keyed the mic again barking for Jack or Kai to answer. A static-filled voice responded. It was Jack.

"Sorry, Pop. Meant to call in but got tied up. The radio was in my pocket."

"What are you guys doin'? I told you to stay in touch every ten minutes. You haven't even gone ashore."

"Yeah, I know. We were talking about the search. Calico Jack was explaining some stuff and we lost track of time."

"Well get movin'. I'm a sittin' duck out here."

They walked through a thicket toward the northern edge of the little island where they found a weathered coral rock half buried in sand. It was the size of a small car.

"Here we be, lads."

"Here we be where?" grumped Kai. "You're not sayin' this great fortune is buried under a freakin' rock, I hope."

"Indeed I am."

"And you think it's still here after all this time. No one would have noticed that this rock is out of place and poked around to check it out."

"Trust me."

Kai shook his head in disgust. "Care to explain how we move this thing?"

Calico Jack walked to the opposite side. "If ye pull the sand away from the base over here, 'twill move with surprisin' ease."

The boys knelt and shoveled alongside the rock with their hands. Jack explained to Pop that they had reached their destination, but offered nothing more. He couldn't mention anything specific over the radio, in case someone caught their conversation over the airways. After nearly an hour of steady digging, sweating, and Kai's nonstop complaints, they paused at the sound of a low rumble below their feet. As promised, the rock rolled away exposing heavy timbers.

Kai stared at the pirate and pointed at the wood planks. "Are you gonna help with these or just watch like you did when we were diggin'?"

Calico Jack laughed. "Allow me." He walked to the center of the wooden square, and turned facing east with one foot on the sand. "Stand back." He drew his cutlass, thrust it between the outermost planks to his right, and pushed the blade to the hilt. A metallic sound followed before the boards swung downward into a dark hole. "We'll be needin' a torch."

Jack rummaged through the knapsack and produced a pair of high-powered flashlights. He flicked them on and handed one to Kai. "Want to do the honors?" he asked pointing to the opening at their feet.

"Nah, I'll bring up the rear. Check this out. Steps."

"Me men stacked stones and mortared them together. No tellin' their condition, after all this time, so take great care."

"Everything's probably under water. We should get our scuba gear," said Jack.

"This leads to a cavern. At high tide, the steps shall be covered, but at present we will be in water only waist deep. 'Tis a short slog to the hideout. Not to worry, 'tis never fully submerged."

Jack took a deep breath. His legs shook as he climbed down the stacked stones. Partway down, in water up to his knees, he stopped to report to Pop that they were going inside and might lose contact for a while.

X

The boys waded deeper into the underground tunnel through seawater that was closer to chest level. They could hear the sound of the ocean behind them and dripping noises ahead. There was no sign of Calico Jack.

"Where's you-know-who?" asked Kai.

"He's probably shoving the rock over the hole to trap us in here forever."

"Great and the tide's coming in."

"There's an opening ahead and it's going uphill from here. We'll be fine."

"Yeah, right. Fine."

Jack toppled forward landing hard against square shaped rocks. Another set of steps. He rubbed his elbow and turned, aiming the flashlight toward the entrance from the beach. The water had risen six inches in less than ten minutes. Movement to his left caught his attention and he turned the light in time to catch a glimpse of moray eel slithering in their direction. He grabbed Kai by the arm and tugged. "Hurry, there's an eel scoping us out. He's about twelve feet long and has a mouthful of razor sharp teeth."

Kai made it through the opening first. "Did you really see an eel or were you tryin' to make me hurry?"

"Both."

"Great. Somethin' to look forward to on the return trip." Kai pulled himself into a crouch and moved into the tunnel. They were now ankle deep in water. A pungent odor filled the passage and burned their eyes. They continued forward another fifty yards before they could stand. The smell weakened and they gulped for air.

"This might be the dumbest thing we've ever done," said Jack.

"It's gotta be in the top three," agreed Kai. "Look, skulls. Human ones. Must be a dozen of 'em. This gets better by the minute." Kai knelt and picked up the top half of one of the skulls, the jaw section no longer attached.

"Must be somebody who tried to get the treasure," said Jack.

"How much you want to bet it's the guys that buried it in the first place?"

"Kai is quite correct, Jack. As I said lad, ye would have made a fine pirate."

"Where'd you come from?" asked Kai.

"I didn't see the need to take the same route as it seemed quite impossible for either of ye to get lost. Did ye meet me eel on the way?"

"You sent the eel?"

"'Twas turning into a most dreadful long wait."

"And these skeletons were your men?" asked Jack.

"Remember the story of the rat eaters?"

"You said you didn't kill them," said Kai. "You lied."

"I said we put them ashore an' here they be, along with some others. Aye, built the hideaway they did, but it wouldn't do to have those lubbers escapin' to go struttin' about an' tellin' me secret. Ye lads must see me logic in that. They had a store of rations an' rats o' plenty. Ye be standin' an' walkin' through the cay's only fresh water supply."

"You buried them alive."

"Think what ye will. We've work to do an' sundown is fast approaching. Follow me gentlemen." Calico Jack Rackham turned and glided into the gloom. His boots hovered six inches above the water as he moved.

~19~
CAVERN CURSE

RACHEL TRIED TO RELAX in the light breeze sitting at the water's edge in a padded chaise lounge between Flo and Val. Nan busied herself further down the beach, taking pictures of shells and seabirds. Val noticed Rachel's restlessness.

Rachel, sensing Val's stare, turned to face her. "When will they be back?

"You miss Jack?"

"Well, yeah. I think we should have gone along and pitched in."

Flo looked up from her magazine. "Mr. Rackham did not think it safe, child. He has worried that the men following were a threat. He would never want harm to come to his friends and family."

"Jack's family, so is Kai, sort of."

"Yes but the boys are big and strong. You are but a tiny wisp of a girl."

"I'm tough enough. I still say we should have gone to help."

"I could take you in the plane and try to find them if you would like," said Flo.

"No thanks, Flo. I'm still shaky from the last ride."

"Rachel, are you alright?" Nan had returned from her walk. "You look awful. Didn't you sleep well last night?"

"I'm fine."

"Well, you have dark circles under very bloodshot eyes."

"Honestly, I didn't sleep very much."

"Is there something wrong with your bed or the pillows? Do you want me to have Felix move you to another cottage?" asked Flo.

Rachel smiled. "Flo, everything about the cottage is fantastic. I just had a terrible nightmare and when I woke up, I found myself standing on the dock where *Reckless* should have been tied off."

"Do you remember what the nightmare was about?" asked Val.

"I don't think I want to talk about it. You'll all think I'm crazy."

"We like crazy. Come on tell us. No one will laugh."

Rachel sighed. "Okay, but it's really strange. I saw two men in a small boat pull alongside *Reckless*. One man was saying something to Pop and then pulled out a gun and shot him. Then there was this dark tunnel, and Jack and Kai were walking through it, past skulls and skeletons and something that looked like a snake with teeth. They reached a big cave and this horrible looking man was waiting for them in the shadows. He wore very strange clothes and his eye dangled out of the socket against his cheek. His hands and neck were bloody and raw and he reached out and grabbed Jack by the arm and…when Jack yelled and fell down, I woke up."

Nan tried to hide the worry that she felt. "It was just a bad dream, Rachel. Don't get yourself all upset. Jack's tough. He can take care of himself."

"Nan's right. Everything's cool. You ought to try to get some sleep," said Val.

Flo placed a hand on Rachel's arm. "Come with me. I will have Felix and Marguerite set up a lovely cabana in the shade of the palms in the gardens facing the beach. You will enjoy the whisper of the waves and the songs of the birds while you rest."

"How can I resist that? You're spoiling me, Flo."

Rachel followed Flo toward the gardens. Nan waited until they were gone and said to Val, "I'm going to call Pop on the radio and make sure everything's okay."

"You think something happened?"

"No, but it won't hurt to see what's up."

Rachel's head barely touched the pillow before she fell into a fitful sleep, the sound of the surf replaced by an evil whisper, gruff and desperate.

Jack and Kai entered the cavern. Torches blazed, stuck within the fissures of the cave's wall. Calico Jack Rackham stood in the shadows and motioned them forward.

"Geez, look at this stuff, there must be a ton of gold in here," said Kai.

"Maybe more," said Jack. "How're we getting all of this out of here?

"'Tis all yers me hearties, once ye find the jeweled dagger of King Quetzalcoatl."

"The jewel of what?" asked Kai.

"Quetzalcoatl. The blonde blue eyed Aztec. In the midst of this booty, ye will find a magnificent dagger of gold. The handle be cast in the image of a feathered serpent with a clear green stone centered in 'is belly known as the Wind Jewel."

"You know what it looks like, you find it," said Kai.

"'Tis the least ye can do for me," said the pirate.

"Why is this dagger so important? What does it do for you?" asked Jack.

"'Twas me most prized possession it was."

"That makes no sense. If it were that important, you wouldn't have left it behind. There's something you're holding back."

"Jack, what's the big deal about a lousy knife?" asked Kai.

"Maybe nothing. I say we at least load this gold onto our boat before we give him the dagger."

Calico Jack's eyes blazed and his jaw tightened. "Ye still don't trust me, young Jack."

"Why should I? We passed some of your former shipmates on our way through the tunnel."

"Ye have me oath that me interest ends with the dagger. Proceed with the task. Me patience wears thin, but me intentions will soon be known."

"Kai, this is going to take days to haul all of this through that tunnel. We need to tell Pop what we've got here."

"'Twill not be so difficult as that." Calico Jack removed his cutlass and, as he did at the planking at the entrance, shoved the blade into a crevice up to the hilt and pushed the blade downward. The wall of the cavern creaked outward a few inches. "Bring both vessels to the leeward side of the island while the tide is high an' ye can make short work o' this task."

Jack walked to the gap in the stone. "Give me a hand, Kai." The boys leaned their shoulders into the rock and pushed the coral far enough to squeeze through. Once outside, they cleared the sand from the base of the rock, creating wide-open access to the pirate's hiding place. "How about if you go get Pop. I want to talk to Calico Jack."

"I don't think it's a good idea hangin' out with a dead guy all alone," said Kai.

"It'll be okay. He's holding back some kind of secret. Before we haul the stuff out of here, I need to find out what it is."

"Pop said to stay together."

"Just go get him."

"Well, he's gonna be mad at me now. Better talk fast, 'cause I won't be gone long," said Kai as he stomped off.

Jack returned to the cavern and faced the dead pirate. "Tell me about the dagger. Why do you need it?"

Calico Jack sneered. "'Tis me secret to keep."

"What if we don't give it to you?"

"Come here an' let me show ye,"

"Think I'll stay put for now."

"Ye recall me ability to control minds, the same gift I so generously offered ye?"

"Yeah, think I'll pass on that too," said Jack.

The pirate walked toward Jack, "Give me your hand."

"Just stay where you are."

"Fascinatin', m'lad. Me mind can no longer enter yours. Ye have a strong will, young Rackham." With two strides, the pirate closed the gap and grabbed Jack by the right forearm. "Watch and learn," said Calico Jack.

Jack's arm burned, steam rising from beneath the pirate's grasp. As the grip tightened, the pain exploded and the arm sizzled causing Jack to collapse to both knees. Finally, Calico Jack released his hold. The smell of burnt flesh filled the air as Jack rolled onto his back into the wet muck of the cave's floor, hyperventilating, struggling to maintain consciousness. Several minutes passed before his pulse slowed and head cleared. Jack gritted his teeth as he looked down at his maimed arm, the skin now branded with the swollen and bloody outline of a skull with crossed cutlasses, the emblem of Calico Jack Rackham.

Kai pulled alongside *Reckless* and tossed a line up to Pop. He clambered up the rope ladder and stood breathless on the deck. "We found it. There's a ton of gold ingots and statues," said Kai.

"Where's Jack?"

"In the cave with Calico Jack."

"Why'd you leave him alone with…"

"Jack told me to come get you. We have to go to the opposite side of the island to pick up the stuff. There's a secret exit that opened up right at the edge of the beach."

"I told you guys to stay together."

"I know. He wouldn't listen to me."

Pop shook his head. "Tie *Bad Latitude* off at the stern, we'll tow her to the leeward side. I'll weigh anchor and we'll get underway. Should've gone ashore with you chuckleheads in the first place."

"He's fine, Pop."

"We'll see. I have a bad feeling about this."

Rachel stirred. She was hearing that awful voice again.

"Leave this island or they will all die."

In her mind, she could see Jack. He was in pain, clutching his arm as the man with the hanging eyeball peered down at him.

"I will kill him first. You will watch him die an agonizing death."

She sat up and looked around. Her heartbeat drowned out all sound.

"He is dying now. Only you can save him. Leave the island and I will spare him."

Rachel stood, struggling to keep her balance. She could still see Jack writhing in agony. She had to save him. Leaving the island with no one seeing her was the only way.

Nan and Flo chatted together on the beach. Val floated on a bright pink raft in middle of the swimming pool. Rachel hurried to the cottage, trying to avoid attention. The voice continued in her head, piercing her ears. She slammed the door shut, leaning against the wall, sobbing hysterically. After a few minutes, she collected herself and scribbled a short note.

> *I am so sorry to have to leave. It's for the best. Thank you for everything.*
>
> *Love,*
> *Rachel*

Her battered tan bag hung from a hook in the closet. She grabbed it by the strap, her last link to her past. After chang-

ing clothes, she walked to the screen door and peered outside; making sure no one could see her. With a deep breath,
she ran toward the marina. The voice and the vision of Jack
played nonstop in her mind.

～20～
THE SERPENT DAGGER

⁓JACK STOOD FACE TO FACE WITH CALICO JACK. His legs felt rubbery, his arms limp and weak. "What did you do to me?"

"I have given you the power to alter the thinkin' of others did I."

"Told you I didn't want it. Take it back."

"Ah, frightened are we."

"Of what?"

"Power, m'lad, power. 'Tis in yer very grasp an' with me help n' guidance, ye can make yer fortune an' I shall have me heart's desire. No mortal man can stop us once…"

"Once I give you the dagger with the Wind Jewel of Quetzalcoatl," Jack finished.

"Such a great mind ye have."

"The secret is that I have to hand it to you for it to work. It must be given, not taken."

Calico Jack was stunned. "Give me the icon."

"After we load the gold aboard *Reckless*."

"Fair enough, but be warned, I shall have the dagger before sundown."

"What kind of power will this dagger give you that you don't already have? It can't bring you back to life."

"No, me life is ended, 'tis true enough, an' that shall not change, in this age."

"Then, what's the point?"

The pirate paused, carefully choosing his words. "'Twill give me the chance to start again and be…"

"Be what?"

"The man I could have been. Quiet now, young Kai and Mr. Rackham approach. Keep silent, for the sake of their very lives."

Jack nodded, knowing that Pop and Kai were now in danger. He reached down to cover the burn on his forearm, but there was no trace of the Rackham brand.

Pop and Kai rushed into the cavern a few seconds later.

"Thought I told you two to stay together," barked Pop.

"Yer grandson was never in peril, Mr. Rackham."

"You mind your business. When I have somethin' to say to my grandson, you keep quiet."

"As ye wish, sir. I shall see ye aboard the schooner shortly." Calico Jack faded into the tunnel.

"You okay?" asked Kai. "He didn't try any of that mind control crap, did he?"

"I'm fine. Sorry, Pop, I thought it made sense to stay here to keep an eye on things. Guess I should've listened."

"Yeah, maybe. Geez, Kai, you weren't kiddin', there must be a ton of gold sittin' here." Pop walked over to the treasure, picking up gold ingots and statuary, carefully inspecting them. This is Aztec gold."

"It's from the treasure of Quetzalcoatl," said Jack.

"How would you know that?" asked Pop.

"Uh, Calico Jack told me."

"Tell him about the snake knife," said Kai.

"Let's get the stuff out of here first," answered Jack.

"Steak knife?" asked Pop.

"Snake. S-N-A-K-E. There's a dagger in here that Calico Jack wants. The handle looks like a snake with feathers or wings. We have to keep it from him until we get all of this loaded onto *Reckless*. I think it was used for some kind of ancient ceremony and has some kind of power that he needs to exist."

"Let's find the dagger first. I'll hang onto it while we load the boat," said Pop. "After that, we'll decide how to deal with Calico Jack."

Kai found the dagger wrapped in a disintegrating Spanish flag at the bottom of the pile. It was a magnificent creation, a golden serpent with a round green jewel in the center, a stone that even Pop couldn't identify. Pop tucked the weapon inside his shirt.

The intensity of the voice escalated as Rachel climbed into the skiff. Her head throbbed and her breathing came in labored gasps while her vision blurred.

"*Hurry, lass. His time is nearly finished. Only you can save him.*"

The boat's motor started and she tossed the spring line to the deck before spinning the bow toward the middle of the lagoon and Flo's yellow seaplane. Val's muffled voice carried down the gangway toward the water.

As the last of the ingots were stowed, Calico Jack appeared at the stern. "Gentlemen, now that the task of securing the Rackham treasure is completed, I should like to collect me prize."

Pop removed the flag covered icon from his waistband and moved to the helm. The pirate stared at the rotted fabric, his tongue making a slow hungry swipe across his upper lip. "Aye, that be the dagger of Quetzalcoatl. Make haste and hand it over, sir."

"First tell us about the importance of this relic," said Pop as he eased into his seat behind the schooner's massive wheel.

"Me explainin' be finished. Give me the blasted ..."

"You're aboard my boat as a guest, Captain Rackham. You don't give the orders here. Now explain your urgent need for this dagger."

Calico Jack's face contorted with rage, turning a shade of vomit green as his eye exploded from its socket. He shoved it back in place, fighting to compose himself. "Have I not kept me word? Have I not made ye wealthy beyond yer dreams this very day?"

"I solved the secret of the plates long before we left port. Your involvement only helped speed things up and besides, we're already wealthy. Now tell me the secret of the dagger."

"Ye will be the last."

"Last?"

"The last to die, Mr. Rackham. Prepared was I for such a turn. The first of yer happy lot is about to join me first, a pretty young lass known as Rachel."

Val propped herself up on her elbows, craning her neck to watch Rachel run toward the little skiff. She called out, but Rachel never slowed. Something was wrong. Val abandoned the raft, swam to the side of the pool, climbed from the water and ran the length of the dock at full speed while she screamed Rachel's name repeatedly. She reached the end of the dock as Rachel motored off in the skiff toward the seaplane.

Tears streamed down Rachel's face as the skiff banged hard against the plane's pontoon. The voice hammered in her head as she untied the plane from its mooring. She climbed into the cockpit and stared at the instrument panel.

"He's down to his last minutes. Ye must flee the island to save his life."

In her mind, Rachel watched Jack crawling across the deck of *Reckless Endeavor*, surrounded by flashes of intense light. He was reaching for something, struggling against a crushing weight, his blue eyes changing to brilliant red. She flipped a bank of switches; unaware of what she was doing and not knowing what she was supposed to do. The engine caught and the propeller spun creating a loud drone, but it didn't drown out the sound of the voice.

Val's screaming attracted the attention of Nan, Flo and Eb's security team. They ran toward the sound and crowded at the end of the dock waving and yelling for Rachel to stop, but it was no use. There was no time to secure a boat to intercept the plane and they watched helplessly as the craft spun wildly through the lagoon. After narrowly missing a pair of jet-skis, the seaplane lifted off, its wings dipping dangerously from side to side before leveling out on its way toward the open sea. Rachel's hands hung limp at her sides as she lapsed into a state of unconsciousness. An unseen menace now controlled the flight.

X

It all happened in seconds.

"What are you talkin' about? What's the matter with Rachel?" hollered Pop.

The dead pirate laughed. "Don't ruin me sport, Mr. Rackham. Usin' me gift of controllin' minds, I have sent young Rachel on a short journey, from which she shall never return. Her tormented spirit will roam the ocean floor searchin' for one last sweet breath, thanks to yer stubbornness."

Without warning, Pop rushed Calico Jack with his hands outstretched, catching the pirate by the throat. Pop clenched his hands on the windpipe, squeezing with all his strength. His fingers sank into a mass of rotted wet tissue, and slipped through the back of the corpse's skull, dripping a snot-like liquid. Calico Jack's face turned a deeper shade of green as he grabbed Pop by the face, ready to snap the old man's neck.

Kai and Jack flung themselves at Calico Jack. The pirate slammed Pop to the deck to fend them off. He grabbed Kai in a fierce headlock as he kicked Jack in the face, sending him reeling backwards onto the deck next to Pop.

"Sadly, lad, it be yer turn, to join Miss Rachel. Ye would have made such a fine buccaneer."

Jack jumped to his feet. "I'll give you the dagger. Let him go."

"Don't do it, Jack," Kai croaked, still fighting to escape.

"I'll be makin' me point if ye don't mind. Ye had yer chance." Calico Jack yanked Kai by the hair, pulling his face within inches of his own. "It's me understandin' that ye have a terrible scar from a shark attack, m'boy. I think that shall be the death I choose for ye."

The pirate lifted Kai with his right hand and stretched out his left across the gunwale, squeezing it into a fist. Blood spurted from between his fingers into the aqua-blue waters below. Ten seconds passed before the frenzied sharks arrived. "Aye, a fine pirate indeed, such a waste," said Calico Jack as he lifted Kai over the side.

Jack dove past the pirate and grabbed Kai by the shirt as Calico Jack released his grip, leaving Kai to dangle with his feet kicking inches above the water and Jack leaning across the gunwale beyond his waist, hanging on to his friend, refusing to let go.

"Such loyal mates," scoffed Calico Jack as he pulled his cutlass from its scabbard. He leaned over the side taking aim at Jack's arm.

⌒21⌒
DEAD AHEAD, DEAD AGAIN

⌒FLO, DO YOU KEEP THE RADIO turned on in the plane?" asked Nan.

"Always. I'll try to reach her from the boat shed. Eb, call the Bahamas Air Sea Rescue and give them the tail number. She was heading southwest, hopefully she hasn't changed course." Eb hurried toward the office. Val hung close to Nan.

Rachel remained slumped, semi-conscious in the seat leaning against the door of the plane. There was a new voice in the background. It had changed, squeaky, not deep and raspy, accompanied by static, familiar, not threatening. She stirred, blinking her eyes against the orange glow of the sun ahead. Her head ached and her mouth felt dry. Why was she hearing Flo?

A rough pass through an air pocket erased the brain fog when her head banged against the hatch window. It WAS Flo's voice squawking Rachel's name. Panic took over when Rachel realized she was alone in a plane, several hundred feet above the water, with no idea how she had gotten there and worse, how she would get down. Her eyes darted around the cabin, looking for the source of Flo's voice. She screamed.

"Let go, Jack," yelled Kai.

"Hang on!" Jack yanked upward as the cutlass swished through the air, slicing through Kai's shirt. Jack stumbled backward, slamming hard against the helm as Kai splashed into the sea.

Blood from a deep gash across his scalp poured down Pop's face, making it impossible to see out of his right eye. He crawled to his knees while reaching for the golden dagger. As Calico Jack swung the cutlass toward Jack's arm, Pop lunged with the dagger. He was a moment too late to save Kai.

Rachel fumbled with the microphone, finally pulling it loose from its clip on the side of the radio. She clicked the send button. "Help me," she cried.

Nan leaned closer to Flo. "It's Rachel, she's alive!"

Flo keyed the mike, and spoke in a controlled tone. "Rachel, are you okay? Can you give us any idea about where you are?"

Rachel twisted in her seat, looking out the windows. "I'm scared. I don' know where I am or how I got here and all I see is water everywhere."

"Okay. What is your heading, I mean, direction? Look at the compass in the center of the, uh, dashboard."

"It says southwest."

"Good. Now stay calm and I'll talk you through this to explain how things work. Everything will be fine." Flo looked at Nan and shrugged. "Let's start with the instrument panel."

"Now I see land straight ahead. There's a bridge. Looks like there's more than one bridge."

"Can you look at the GPS and read the numbers to me? There will be two and that will pinpoint your location."

Rachel took a deep breath. "Okay. I see 25.16 and 80.38."

Flo traced her finger across a chart spread over the table and sighed. "Key Largo. She's about to cross Key Largo."

Nan stared down to where Flo pointed. "There's nowhere for her to bring it down unless you can teach her how to turn around."

"And there's no time for that, she's almost out of fuel."

"How do you know that?" asked Nan.

"She traveled at top speed and the plane's fuel tank was only a quarter-full. At most, Rachel can stay airborne for only fifteen minutes, maybe less. I can get her to throttle back and descend, but she can't last long enough to learn to use the plane's rudder. The only choice now is to get her low and slow."

"Where will she end up if she doesn't change course?"

Rachel interrupted. "Flo, Nan, did you guys forget about me?"

"No, baby, just getting a location so we can get you some help. You've got to remain calm and listen very carefully. Do exactly as I say."

Val looked at the chart from the opposite side of the table. "The everglades."

"What did you say, Val?" asked Nan.

"She's on course to crash in the everglades."

Pop put every ounce of energy into his attack on Calico Jack, thrusting the ceremonial dagger through the pirate's chest, embedding the weapon to the hilt until the knuckles of his own fingers slammed against the villain's spine. He peered through the dripping blood from his own wound into the startled face of the famous buccaneer before twisting the blade and shoving the corpse to the deck. As Calico Jack collapsed in a heap, Pop limped to the gunwale looking for the floating remains of Kai. He left the dagger protruding from the pirate's chest.

Jack, holding his side, convinced that his ribs were broken, joined Pop at the gunwale and patted him on the back.

"It's my fault," said Pop as he wiped the blood from his face. "I just had to go after one more pile of treasure and now Kai's dead."

"What makes you think he's dead? Remember the mind control trick? Calico Jack could have made us think we were seeing sharks, like he did with me."

"No, I heard the splashin' and the scream at the same time you went flyin' through the air toward the helm. He's gone this time."

Jack shook his head. "I think you're wrong." As he said the words, he clutched at his forearm, gasping with pain. The flesh on his arm swelled revealing the raised red brand of the Rackham symbol. "He's not dead, Pop."

"Okay, okay, so he's not dead…what's wrong with your arm?"

"Calico Jack's not dead," yelled Jack through clenched teeth. "This is his mark. Geez, it burns." He held his arm out for Pop to see.

Rachel closed the throttle down gently and reported her RPMs and air speed to Flo as instructed. The nose of the small plane tilted downward, as the altimeter registered the decreasing altitude. What a way to go, she thought. After persevering through so many tragedies during her sixteen years, Rachel was going to die alone in a plane crash. She had given up trying to figure things out. The fuel gauge mocked her from the control panel. Not long now she thought, as she crossed above Key Largo. Next stop, according to Flo, would be the everglades, a place teeming with alligators, snakes and insects. If the crash didn't kill her, she would probably be eaten alive by some swamp creature crawling or slithering below. She shivered at the thought and keyed the mic to report her altitude and speed to Flo one more time. If she was going to die, might as well sound confident over the radio. At least Jack would believe she had been brave at the very end.

Jack noticed movement behind Pop and shoved him aside. He dove to the deck, tackling the writhing pirate as the corpse pulled at the dagger lodged in its chest. The pirate's skin dripped from his bones, steam rising as body fluids leaked, forming a large pool where he had collapsed. The pair struggled, each grappling for control of the golden icon. Jack smashed his elbow into what was left of the pirate's face, shattering the bone before ripping the dagger, along with half of Calico Jack's right arm, from the decomposing torso.

Pop dragged Jack away from the pirate's remains as Jack held onto the arm. "You okay?"

"I think so."

Kai climbed over the gunwale, dripping seawater all over the deck. "That sucked. You guys worried about me?"

Jack shook his head and pointed toward the disintegrating corpse. "We kinda had our hands full. How was your swim with the sharks?"

"All an illusion, I think."

"Whaddya mean you think?"

"Soon as I hit the water, I swam behind the keel, kicked off from there and jumped onto your boat. Hardly in the water long enough to get wet. No sense taking a chance, in case they were real. Uh, what's that?"

"It's what's left of Calico Jack's arm. It snapped off at the elbow when I was trying to get the dagger."

Pop leaned over and pried the pirate's arm from Jack's grip. "Think I can get rid of this now? Gives me the creeps." He laid the arm on the deck near the stern, the gruesome hand still latched onto the dagger's handle.

"Sure. Let's wrap some anchor chain around it. Make sure it goes to the bottom."

"Dagger too?"

"Guess so."

"I think that would be a mistake. The arm yeah, but the dagger has some kind of mystic power. We ought to lock it away so no one can ever get to it again," suggested Kai.

"How about we dump it at the edge of the underwater cliff near Bimini? No one will ever find it a mile deep," said Jack.

"No, Kai's right. We can't throw it overboard before finding out what it does and why Calico Jack wanted it so badly," said Pop.

"Okay, so what about the corpse. Bag it up, weight it down and drop it near Bimini?"

"The way it's melting away, there probably won't be anything left to dump overboard."

"I just want to make sure he's gone for good." As Jack uttered the words, he spun toward the sound of clattering from the stern, in time to see the arm crawl to the center of the puddle that was now Calico Jack.

Pop, Kai and Jack watched helplessly as the fluids and tissues on the deck boiled and swirled together, pulsing into hideous shapes, finally attaching to the hideous arm. In moments, Calico Jack Rackham stood before them, the dagger in his right hand, and a cutlass in his left.

"Our business remains unfinished, young Jack," said the pirate.

"The only business left for me is to kill you, for good this time."

"Aye, we shall see, lad." With that, Calico Jack disappeared.

Kai was first to break the silence. "Looks like you scared him off."

"He's got the dagger, so I don't know what he's after now."

Pop walked over to where Calico Jack had stood. He bent down, retrieved something from the deck, and turned to face the boys. "You can count on another visit sometime soon. He left this behind." Between his thumb and index finger, Pop held out the Wind Jewel which had fallen from the handle of the golden dagger.

"Maybe we should throw THAT overboard," said Kai.

Jack leaned against the gunwale accepting the gemstone from Pop. "No, I have a feeling this is going to come in handy. Besides, I want one more shot at Calico Jack."

The radio at the helm screeched, Nan's voice was barely audible through the static. Pop crossed to the panel, adjusted the squelch button and answered the call. "Is everything okay," he asked.

"No, not even close," she replied. "Rachel took off in Flo's plane; she's headed southwest toward land."

"Since when could she fly?"

"She can't! Rachel told me over the radio that she doesn't even remember how she got on the plane, like she blacked out and then found herself in the air."

"You're in touch with her?"

"Flo's been back and forth with her on the radio, they're on channel 8."

"Can Flo talk her down safely?"

"No. The seaplane is too low on fuel and there's no time for practice runs. Flo worried that if Rachel tried to use the rudder she would go into a spin and crash in the ocean. Right now she's headed for the everglades so Flo's getting her to reduce speed and altitude. Hopefully, she can get low and slow enough that the impact won't make the plane break apart. The Coast Guard is already working on getting a fix on her probable crash site based on Flo's estimate of Rachel's speed and direction."

Jack joined Pop at the helm, listening to Nan as she explained Rachel's dilemma. He knew Calico Jack had used mind control on Rachel as a means to get Jack to do the pirate's bidding. Now that Calico Jack had the dagger, Rachel's fate was sealed. He opened his fist and stared down at the Wind Jewel, then at the brand on his forearm. Maybe there was still a way. He closed his eyes and concentrated while the painful brand on his arm glowed and pulsed.

~22~
CRASH LANDING

⌐THE WHINE OF THE SMALL PLANE'S engine changed to a lower pitch with the throttle cut back. The ride turned bumpier, a rock ready to drop. "Flo, it won't be long now, the fuel's almost gone and the engine is sounding kinda funny," announced Rachel.

"Your airspeed will continue to decrease, Rachel. You need to get that bird low enough to almost touch the tree tops," said Flo. "It's your only chance. When the engine cuts out, don't panic, keep it steady and hopefully you will glide into some small pines or mangroves."

Jack's concentration was total. Pop and Kai tried to get his attention but all he could hear was the sound of an engine. He found himself looking through the windshield of a plane, watching as it descended toward a massive swamp. Hands blocked his vision. It was Rachel, using her hands to cover her face, Flo's voice now echoed in the distance. The plane's engine sputtered several times and then quit. In his mind, he tried to reach the controls, but it was no use. He didn't know how to use the power that Calico Jack had infected him with.

Rachel peeked between her fingers at the sound of the engine shutting down. The plane wobbled, heading downward toward a stand of pines. She pulled back on the controls, trying to keep the nose up. A larger wooded area lay ahead; the plane would never clear the taller trees. She felt an odd presence in the cockpit, but the passenger seat was empty. After a deep breath, she clicked the microphone. "Flo, this is it. The engine quit and I'll be down in a few seconds. Looks like I'll crash in some thicker woods up ahead, not too much water. Lots of grass. Looks like a small river over to my right. Tell everyone I…"

Jack watched it all happen in slow motion. The right wing caught against a pine, causing the plane to spin sideways before upending into a cartwheel motion followed by a violent thud. Everything went black.

He was flat on his back on the deck next to the doorway of the cabin. Kai and Pop were kneeling beside him, shaking him and yelling something. They sounded distant. Jack propped himself up on his elbows, a vacant look on his face. His neck and back hurt. "What happened?"

"You scared the crap out of us," yelled Kai.

"Jack, you had some kind of seizure. It was almost like you were in some sort of trance. Then you started screamin' and thrashin' around on the deck. We had to hold you down for your own good," explained Pop.

"Rachel's plane crashed," said Jack in a whisper. "I think she's dead."

"We know that her plane went down out in the everglades, but we don't know if she's dead, so don't go jumpin' to conclusions," said Pop.

Jack looked up at his grandfather and realized, for the first time, that Pop looked old and worn out. "I was on the plane with Rachel when it crashed. I saw it happen, felt the spinning, heard the metal tearing apart, and then… and then everything went dark and quiet."

"You were here on the boat the whole time."

"It's the mind stuff," said Kai. "Calico Jack cursed 'im with that mind control thing so Jack was in Rachel's brain when she crashed. Right Jack?"

"I think so."

"You're tellin' me you can control people's minds? Is that what that skull thing on your arm is all about?" Pop's breathing was coming in short gasps and his hands shook.

"Maybe. The thing is, I don't know how to use it, Pop. I don't even want to use it. He grabbed my arm and burned his mark on me. Finding myself on that plane, mentally anyway, just happened but I let her down when she needed me the most."

"You're nuts. Whaddya think you could've done?" asked Kai.

"I don't know. Tell me how I got there in the first place."

"You were listenin' to Nan and somehow willed yourself to be there, I guess," said Pop. "Maybe what you saw will help us find her."

Jack looked around *Reckless*. All signs of the struggle with Calico Jack Rackham were gone but something was wrong. "Why are we sailing west? Shouldn't we head toward the Keys so we can start searching?"

"We're goin' back to Eb and Flo's to get Nan and Val. It's gonna be dark soon. We're gonna sail through the night, should arrive at Largo a couple hours before daybreak. Flo's tryin' to figure out our search zone coordinates based on, uh, guesswork about where Rachel was when she ran out of fuel," said Pop.

"So if Rachel survived the crash, now she's going to have to make it through the night in the middle of a huge swamp."

"Well, yeah, that's about right. Sorry, Jack, just don't know what to say to make you feel better. No on can search at night, including us. Try to stay positive."

"Maybe you should try makin' contact with Rachel again. Practice that mind readin' stuff," suggested Kai.

"Think it'll work?"

"It's worth a try."

Twilight settled in and Jack paced alone around the schooner's bow. They were two hours from port and Rachel's plane remained lost. The Coast Guard search would soon end for the night. Dizzy. Everything swirled, slowly at first. The sound of the wind and waves became distant and finally, all was silent. Staring past the bowsprit, the sea disappeared, replaced with a blurred vision of broken glass, palm branches and a radio microphone dangling from somewhere above. The breeze stopped. Sweat poured across his face and down his chest as the air turned hot and damp. Steady rhythmic calls of frogs and insects intensified, changing pitches, interrupted by strange buzzing, flapping wings and faraway splashes. Water was close by, but the smell of the sea had vanished, replaced by something pungent, the sour and unpleasant odor of decay, a rotting carcass or swamp mud. Jack's forearm burned as the scar, once again, glowed red. The skull and crossed cutlasses pulsed faster as Jack squeezed his fist tighter, fighting against the pain, fixing his total concentration on Rachel, willing himself to be with her.

Breathing hurt, but she was alive. Rachel rubbed her hand across her face. It was sticky with blood from a cut at her hairline. Twisted sideways, still belted in her seat, she struggled to free herself but the plane's cockpit was leaning to one side and, with her weight pressed against the shoulder harness there was no slack in the belt for her to pry the safety catch open. She noticed that the wings were gone. The windshield had collapsed inward, the space filled with pointy palmetto fronds that had missed her face by inches. It would be full dark soon. She had to get loose. Rachel lifted herself by pulling on the strap bracket at the cockpit wall, enough to release the clasp, and tumbled hard against the bent doorframe. Still dazed, she paused for a few deep breaths. She was sore, but nothing seemed broken. The shattered windshield provided the only route for escape and she pulled herself toward the opening.

Jack watched through Rachel's eyes from the deck of *Reckless Endeavor*. The palm branches parted as Rachel climbed through the windshield. The sounds of night creatures echoed louder. She was pulling herself across the crushed nose of the seaplane. Tumbling. He was looking at thick saw grass. She must have fallen through the canopy of fronds. Her tan bag was on the ground.

Why did she have that ratty bag with her?

Crawling toward it.

Come on, Rachel, just stand up. Forget the stupid bag. Get to the trees, away from the swamp.

He watched her hand grab the worn out strap. She stopped, looking into the grass in front of her. There was movement, the grass parted as it rustled. Something had locked onto her scent. A predator had found her.

Go! Go! There's no time.

He saw it at the same time Rachel screamed. The Python measured at least fifteen feet from its sharp curved teeth to its tail and was more than a foot thick through its middle. The giant snake moved with surprising speed, knocking her backwards, its mouth gaping over her face as it pinned her down. She never had a chance.

The glowing brand on Jack's arm dimmed as he passed out.

~23~
MIND GAMES

RECKLESS WAS ALREADY DOCKED when Jack regained consciousness. Pop or Kai, probably both, had tucked him into the large stateroom. His head was bandaged, an ice pack tucked behind his neck. For the second time, he had failed to save Rachel, the girl who had nothing. Now she was dead. All the gold piled in the hull meant nothing. He would gladly throw it overboard if that could bring her back. Jack rolled onto his side and looked down at the floor. He had crossed the line. Adventure had turned to tragedy. Kai tip-toed into the room and pulled up a chair.

"You okay, Jack?"

"No. And I won't be for a very long time," said Jack in a slow whisper.

"What happened?"

"I watched Rachel die. Saw the whole thing."

"How? She crashed before you tried the mind thing again."

"She survived the crash, Kai. I was with her when she climbed out of the plane. I could see everything the way she saw it as it happened."

"If she climbed out, what makes you think she's dead? Maybe she passed out and you lost the signal. Happens with satellite TV all the time."

"She was attacked by a snake, a really big snake."

"No, I don't believe it."

"Believe it. I was there." Jack held out his arm displaying the now faded Rackham brand. "This curse didn't help me save her. I tried to talk to her through her mind. Tried to tell her to run and get away, but all I could do was watch her die."

Kai's eyes were brimming with tears. His bottom lip trembled as he spoke. "You saw the snake crush her and feed on her body?"

"No. When the snake attacked, it pinned her to the ground, like constrictors do, and moved toward her face to suffocate her. She screamed and fainted before it sunk its teeth into her."

"So you're givin' up now? That's it? You never actually saw her die. You probably just saw her faint. Maybe she got away. Since when did you turn into a quitter?"

"What are you talking about?"

"Try the mind control thing again. Maybe she's okay. Maybe she escaped and she's hidin' out in a tree or somethin'."

"It doesn't work that way, Kai."

"You mean you don't know how it works."

"Look, it's too late. She's gone." Jack sat up on the edge of the bed. "She died a slow painful death and it's my fault."

"So you're not even gonna try."

"No."

"Then it *is* your fault she's dead."

"Yep."

Kai stood up and moved toward the door. "It's funny. I never thought of you as a quitter, 'specially when it comes to people you care about."

"Guess you don't know me as well as you thought."

"Well, I'm outta here. By the way, your grandparents aren't givin' up. They're a complete wreck, but they're flyin' to the Keys at dawn. I'm goin' with 'em, just like I would if it was you lost out there."

"Wait."

"Wait for what? You have this mind thing goin' on and just 'cause you can't make it work the way you want, you're gonna throw in the towel. Jack Rackham, the guy who's always in control, the big risk taker. What's scarin' you so bad?"

"Scared?"

"Yeah. Somethin's not right. What else could it be?"

"You really think she might be alive?"

"Until somebody can prove she's dead, I prefer assumin' the best."

"You sound like Pop."

"Yeah, the old geezer likes that positive thinkin' crap. After awhile, it tends to rub off."

Jack stood up. "Okay, I'll try it."

"Wait. I know what you're afraid of."

"Huh?"

"You're afraid she's hurt really bad, maybe dyin', and you won't be able to find her in time to save her from that slow, painful death."

"Would you want to be eaten alive by a huge snake?"

"I wouldn't want to be eaten alive by anything."

"I'm not scared; just want her to be okay. Let's go topside and give it a shot."

"Maybe you should try it from here. Last time you collapsed and cracked your head. At least there's softer stuff to land on down here."

"I think it might work better outside."

"Nan and Pop are up there. Do you really want to have some kind of convulsions in front of them? They've got enough on their plate."

"Okay, but stay here. If I say anything, try to remember it, even if it doesn't make sense."

"That'll be easy. You don't make sense that often."

Jack looked at the brand on his arm, inhaled deeply and closed his eyes. He felt the room spin and spread his feet to keep his balance. He focused on the mental image of Rachel's face and squeezed his eyes tighter, along with his fists, willing himself to join her in the massive swamp. His heart thundered in his chest as his pulse quickened and his forearm burned. Once again, the orange-red glow of the brand returned. He was traveling, spinning through the gloom.

The sound of rustling vegetation and animal cries pulled him from the darkness. He was there, somewhere in the everglades. His eyes opened, his vision blurred, trained on a fallen tree. There was no movement. He concentrated, trying to make himself heard as he formed the words in his mind. *"Rachel, it's me, Jack. Look around. Let me see through your eyes. Say something. Move around so I can find you. Let me know you're alive."*

"Jack?" Her voice was weak, whisper-like.

"If you can hear me, Kai, I think she's alive. She just called my name."

"That's right, Rachel, it's me. You need to help me find you. Keep talking. Look around."

Rachel was exhausted, barely able to move. Her mind was playing games, it sounded like Jack was nearby, calling out her name, asking her to look around. It was impossible of course, she was alone in the middle of a swamp, and no one could find her in the dark. Still, she propped herself up, leaning her back against a small tree. "Jack, where are you?"

"*I'm trying to find you. Rachel, look around, let me see that you're alright. Trust me, I can see things.*"

She crawled to her knees, and, using the tree for support, pulled herself up until she was standing. Her body ached, and she swayed on her feet. How did she get here? The last thing she remembered was a huge snake wrapping itself around her. Was that just a nightmare? Where was the wrecked plane? Rachel turned her head back and forth, searching through the weakened light from the half-moon. "Jack, I'm scared."

"*I know. You have to be strong and stay alert for a couple more hours until the sun comes up. We're coming to get you but we can't find you in the dark.*"

"Am I really talking to you, Jack, or am I in the middle of a nightmare?"

"*It's a very long story, but this isn't a dream or a nightmare. You're alive and awake and yes, you're really talking to me. I'm communicating with you through your mind and can see everything you can see.*"

"This is too weird. I crashed the plane. I'm in the middle of a swamp. Flo said I was heading for the everglades. When I got out of the plane a snake attacked me, but I don't know how I got away."

"*I saw it all happen, Rachel, and I thought you were dead. I need you to look around. You have to get away from the water. Alligators and snakes feed at night. You have to hide in the trees until morning. Can you walk? Are you hurt bad?*"

"No, just sore. I'm okay enough to walk, Jack, but promise you'll find me. I'm so scared. The noises…"

"I promise. Just stay with me now. Are you near the plane?"
"I don't know."
"Do you see a woods or a bunch of trees nearby? They have to be close but I don't want you to cross through any water."
Rachel turned three hundred and sixty degrees. "Can you see what I see now?"
"Yes. It looks like you found your way out of the swamp grass already. There's a cluster of trees close by, to your left about twenty yards. The ground looks pretty solid, lots of pine needles. Move into that area and settle there for the night. I'll stay with you."
"I wish I had some kind of light. It feels like I'm being watched." Rachel walked toward the stand of trees. "Can't you come find me now?"
"At daybreak, we're going to search from helicopters. Flo has a general idea about where your plane went down. We have no chance of finding you at night."
"I should have stayed in the plane. Maybe I ought to go find it."
"Not now. Did you have to cross through a lot of swamp or water to get to the trees?"
"I don't remember anything after the snake, but my clothes are dry."
"Okay, that's good. We'll find the plane in the morning; it's probably not very far away."
"Jack, I hear something moving this way. It sounds like… someone walking. What should I do?"
"Hide. Try to tuck yourself under some thicket. Look around again so I can see. There. Crawl under those palmettos and be still. Don't talk, not even a whisper."
Rachel scrambled to the edge of the palmettos and eased her way between the fan-like fronds before crouching behind the thicket. She let out a long slow breath, trying to control

her panic. A thin trickle of blood from her scalp dripped down her cheek and she squeezed her eyes shut. The intruder was nearby.

"Rachel, you have to open your eyes so I can see what's happening."

She listened to the cracking sound of branches and forced herself to look. There was nothing to see from the shadows. The noises continued, joined by the sound of humming. "Jack, I think someone is setting up camp here for the night," Rachel whispered.

"Shhhh. It might be a poacher. They hunt alligators at night. Stay put and be quiet."

"Whoever it is, they're building a campfire."

Within a few minutes, Jack could see the light from the flames. Rachel resisted the urge to close her eyes, but didn't turn her head to get a better view. With no breeze stirring the palms, any movement from inside the thicket would make a loud rustling noise and give away her hiding place.

"Hang in there. We're gonna get through this."

Rachel's leg muscles cramped from dehydration and her effort to remain motionless. She could only hope that the hunter wouldn't stay the entire night. Finally, she risked a peek toward the campfire. There was a something skewered on a spit over the fire, but no sign of the person cooking. Maybe they were collecting more firewood. She carefully straightened and stretched her legs a few inches at a time. It seemed to work, the cramping let up and she rolled lightly onto her side, looking for a more comfortable position to hold for the long night ahead.

"Jack, are you there?"

"*Yes, but, Rachel, you have to stay still and completely quiet.*"

"The poacher, or whatever he is, walked into the woods a few minutes ago. It smells like he's cooking something over the fire while he's hunting."

"*Shhh! You have to keep quiet!*"

The trudging sound returned. Rachel squeezed her eyes shut in panic.

"*Open your eyes, Rachel!*"

Reluctantly, she opened them, and found herself staring at a pair of high black boots with brightly colored trousers stuffed into the tops.

⌒24⌒
A NEW QUEST

⌒JACK GASPED AT THE SIGHT of the boots and reached out toward the wall to keep from falling.

"Ah, Miss Rachel, 'tis me pleasure to meet ye at last."

Rachel's eyes moved upward toward the stranger's face. "Who are you? How…"

"Avast, dear girl, I am a longtime observer and friend of the Rackham family. Please, Jack, tell the young lass. I know ye be listenin' and watchin' from that wonderful vessel."

"Jack, what is he talking about?" pleaded Rachel.

"Try to stay calm, he won't hurt you. He wants me."

"'Tis true, m'boy, I'll not do the girl any harm." 'Twas I what saved ye from the bloody snake, lass. Please, Miss, climb from those bushes and refresh yourself with some food and drink. Afraid I've no grog or beef to offer ye, so water and a tasty bit o' rabbit will have to do."

"What should I do, Jack?"

"You might as well do as he says."

"Quite right, me friend. Seems ye have learned to use a part of me gift. Aye, a most impressive accomplishment, lad, and with not the slightest bit of instruction."

Rachel climbed from behind the palmettos and stood. She

stepped backwards as she caught sight of the cutlass and flint-locks tucked loosely at the man's waist. "What do you want?"

"Please, Rachel, take comfort by the fire. Ye can listen to me conversation with Jack. Oh, please, forgive me barbaric manners; I am Calico Jack Rackham, at yer service."

"It's okay, Rachel. He's telling the truth, so far."

"Thank ye, Jack, now let's settle our business."

"Wait a minute. You're saying you're the pirate, Calico Jack Rackham?" asked Rachel.

"Indeed."

"And you're…"

"Dead? Sadly, yes."

Rachel turned and walked away toward the fire and sat down muttering under her breath. After several gulps of water, she rinsed her face and leaned closer to the warmth of the fire, leaving her back turned toward Calico Jack.

"Seems the lass is a might upset. Such a temper for one so…"

Rachel turned. "What do you expect?"

"Dear girl…"

"Stuff the dear girl crap!" Rachel stood and stomped to-ward the pirate. "Today I survived a plane crash and an attack by a huge freakin' snake. The guy I thought would maybe be my boyfriend is talking to me through my head and I'm sit-ting in the middle of the everglades at night having a conver-sation with a corpse. When I get out of here, if I get out of here, I'm jumping on a bus and getting as far away from all of you crazies as I can."

"Rachel, it's okay."

"Jack, if you say that one more time I swear I'll…"

"Rachel, please. Be assured, this lunacy shall make perfect sense, once ye hear me conversation with Jack."

"You're really…dead?"

"Yes. And 'twas truly I what rescued ye from the snake an' carried ye here. Now surely I understand that these events may not be makin' much sense to ye, but…"

Rachel moved to within a foot of the pirate, and stared into his face. Calico Jack leaned back defensively and cocked an eyebrow. She started out calmly before screaming, "This can't be happening. This isn't real. Nothing makes sense. How can anything you idiots say make any sense?" She paused, her eyes widened. "Uh, am I dead?" she asked in a whisper.

"No, Miss Rachel, in fact, ye be quite the live one. Perhaps ye might like to try the rabbit. Would be a shame to waste such a tasty morsel."

"No thanks. Let's hear this conversation that's going to make everything okay." Rachel returned to the fire and sat down, still aching all over.

"Jack, she's so spirited, much like me blessed Anne."

"*What do you want?*" asked Jack.

"Aye, it's with much haste that we get down to our business now is it? Very well. I have the dagger and ye possess the Wind Jewel…"

"*And you want the jewel and the treasure in exchange for Rachel.*"

"Tis not so simple."

"*Thought so. Go on,*" said Jack.

"I'm afraid me strategy was flawed. Never did I imagine that ye would decline me gift of mind control. I daresay I was truly put out by that bit o' pigheadedness, m'lad."

"*So you tried to kill Rachel and Kai? For what? Revenge?*"

Rachel looked up. "You tried to kill me?"

"No, 'twas not me intent at all"

.

"Rachel, he used mind control on you to get to me. That's how you ended up in the plane," said Jack.

"Let me explain. I require the Serpent Dagger and yer most able assistance in gettin' me life back. Yer refusal to bend to me will, and accept the wondrous power I so generously offered, vexed me greatly, and yer confounded stubbornness made it most impossible to control yer thinkin'. Me mistake was explainin' the gift of mind control to ye in the first place. It put ye on guard, which is how ye were able to put up such a resistance to me. When Mr. Rackham plunged the dagger into me chest, a most unfortunate act on his part, I lost control of Miss Rachel's thoughts. The poor girl ended up here while I meself was puttin' me body back together. Melting, ye should know, is nearly as unpleasant as hangin'."

"I can't believe this," said Rachel. "Jack, is he saying you can control minds too?"

Jack ignored Rachel's question. *"What did you really want? If the treasure and the dagger were so important, why did you help us find it? Why not just collect it yourself?"*

"You guys found treasure? Again?" asked Rachel.

"Aye, a king's ransom, dear girl. It now sits in the belly of that magnificent schooner."

"So you want the treasure in exchange for Rachel? You can have it," said Jack.

"Wait a minute, Jack. Is it worth a lot of money?" asked Rachel.

"Yeah, Rachel, a ton of gold is worth millions. There might even be more than a ton."

"You would trade all of that gold for me?" she asked.

"Of course."

Rachel let out a long sigh and smiled.

"Captain, do we have a deal?" asked Jack.

"Not quite, lad, with me apologies. The treasure is all yers. Again, young Rachel shall not be harmed, on that ye have me oath."

"Your oath means nothing. Anything happens to her; I'll hunt you down and kill you again, with my own hands."

"Jack?"

"Stay out of this, Rachel."

"Jack, I think I l…"

"Not a good time, Rachel, but for what it's worth, me too."

"Ah, young love is it? Never-the-less I simply require yer aid in gettin' me life back."

"You've been dead for three hundred years. You're trying to make a deal for something I can't deliver."

"Oh, but ye can. I know the secret, but ye will need the help of another."

"You think?"

"Yes. I have allowed yer friend Kai to listen to our conversation. Ye will need to enlist his able assistance for this task. Kai ye may speak, as all of us shall hear yer reply."

"Uh, this takes weirdness to a whole new level," said Kai. "I think I'll pass."

"Kai, you've heard everything?" asked Jack.

"Sorry to say, yeah. I'm sittin' here in a chair on the boat, watchin' you stare at the wall and listenin' to a conversation like it's coming through earbuds. Your mouth's not even movin'. I'll be in therapy for years after tonight. As far as helpin' you get Calico Jack's life back, count me out. I ain't gettin' into some Frankenstein crap," said Kai.

"I know nothing of this Frankenstein crap," said Calico Jack.

"It's just a story. A mad doctor puts a bunch of parts together from corpses and uses lightning to bring a monster to life. It didn't end well," explained Jack.

"Is such a thing possible in this day and age?"

"No. And if it was, I still wouldn't do it."

"M'lad, I'd ask for nothing like that. Ye must bring me the Wind Jewel and rejoin it with the dagger. I will teach ye in the ways of the powers that ye hold and ye will use that power and the magic of the dagger to rescue me. We have but a fortnight to prepare."

Rachel approached the pirate. "Mr…"

"Please, call me Captain Jack."

"Uh, Captain, uh Jack, what are you asking them to do? Is it something dangerous?"

"'Tis quite dangerous child, but not impossible. I simply want to reclaim me life as a gentleman, raise me son, an' live as a citizen in good standin' with the King. Jack is the only one that can accomplish such a daunting task, gifted as he be."

"Jack, can you hear me?" asked Rachel.

"Yeah, loud and clear."

"Maybe too loud," added Kai.

"Whatever it is you guys have to do, I want to help," said Rachel.

"That's ridiculous. We don't even know what he wants. Besides, I don't trust him."

"Uh, Mr. Calico, this is Kai. You gotta stop talkin' in riddles. What do you want us to do and how do we do it? Maybe we can make a deal."

"Make a deal? He already said it was dangerous. Aren't you getting a little sick of dangerous?" asked Jack.

"I don't know. You're the one that always gets us into these bizarre…"

"I believe, Kai, that a boat filled with gold should suffice as a fair deal, quite generous, in fact."

"I already said we would return it," said Jack.

"The riches mean nothing!" shouted the pirate. He calmed himself before speaking again. "I squandered a life filled with promise. Ye must help me change that, and secure for me a second chance. We must meet at the tomb of Quetzalcoatl. Inside the tomb is a passageway, which leads to the center of time. I will accompany ye to the threshold of me last days, but can venture no further. Once ye cross into me dreaded past, ye will find that I, in that state of time and being, will not know ye and will have no foreknowledge of me fate. Ye must rescue me from the hangman's noose so I may live to spend me days with me dear Ann and the son I never knew."

Rachel's eyes locked into a vacant stare. "You want them to travel back in time."

"Quite right, lass, and must insist that ye accompany me. Our journey begins immediately. Jack, ye shall find Rachel in the Valley of Kings, in the land of the Aztecs on the night of the full moon."

Calico Jack sneered and held the Serpent Dagger in his outstretched hand, pointed toward the night sky, as a green swirling fog rose from the ground, surrounding him. The pirate's evil laugh echoed through the swamp as his face melted away, leaving behind a bleached white skull with a pair of glowing red eye sockets.

Rachel screamed and all went black.

www.ingramcontent.com/pod-product-compliance
Lightning Source LLC
Chambersburg PA
CBHW071508110726
47908CB00003B/763